Sarah Zane

Under Lock & Key

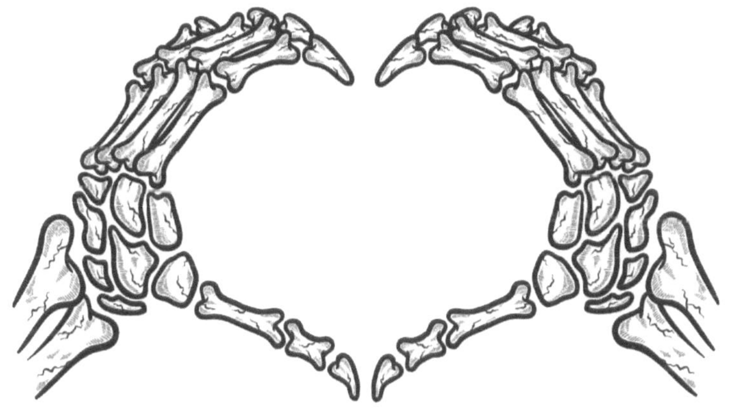

THE SIX REALMS OF
ZANARIA
GLACIAN MOUNTAINS
BANCROFT
OCHRANA MOUNTAINS
MIRAWOOD FOREST
MIRAVALE
SHERBROOKE
VERLASIAN DESERT
SHIMMERING SANDS OASIS
ALTEA
ZANARIAN OCEAN
SANTERRAN SEA
SOMERSET
SANTERRA

For Jess, who didn't laugh at me when I said I wanted to write a sapphic cozy Bluebeard retelling.
Thank you for being you.

Chapter One

I barely suppressed a groan as the latest guests waltzed by, acting like they owned the place. A couple of older women who turned up their noses at me. I couldn't decide if it was the neckline of my dress or the fact that I had the audacity to own an inn while being a woman, but it hardly mattered.

It amounted to the same thing; people either hated me or were intrigued by me.

I knew their type. They thought that them not having to work for a living made them better than me. They, like so many other people who deigned to stay at my Inn, thought that they were above me and treated me as their servant. If it wasn't for my curse, I would have snapped a long time ago. Hells, if it wasn't for my curse, I would have left a long time ago.

The Rose Lily Inn, in its quaint forgotten corner of Somerset, had called to me. It had felt like home when I first stepped in the doors. It was supposed to be my salvation, but under my management, it had grown and changed to be my cage. Now, the Inn I had been so enchanted by went by a new name, The Sapphire Siren Inn, named for the monster that people said ran the place. Me.

I had tried to keep the old name alive, but the townsfolk were always whispering about the sapphire haired harlot on the hill. When the men started paying attention to me, it didn't matter that I had no interest in them, the women started calling me all sorts of names. I used to hum while I worked, sometimes even sing. That was probably where the children got the siren idea from. The women of the town said I drew their men in. It mattered little how untrue it was, they believed what they wanted and started calling me the Sapphire Siren. After a while, I embraced the name.

It turned out to not be bad for business.

The people that came to stay did so for one of two reasons, necessity or curiosity. I liked the former guests much better than the latter. Those who came from curiosity came to gawk at and whisper about me. No one knew why they were drawn there, even I didn't fully understand it, but most nights, the Inn wasn't without guests.

I used to enjoy running the Inn, used to sing to myself while working and bake cinnamon rolls for the guests, but everything changed after that fateful date, after the curse struck.

The first year of the curse had been an unbearable nightmare with Alanna's murder, quickly followed by Zara's. For a long time, their deaths plagued my memories, haunted by dreams. Thankfully, time dulled the pain. It had been a year now since Zara's murder, and things had gotten easier. I formed a nice routine for myself and again allowed myself to put them both out of my mind as best I could. To my surprise and relief, since Zara, I hadn't felt so much as a stirring of the curse.

I wasn't happy per se, but I was content keeping to myself and trying to make the Inn as much of a home as it could be. While it was never without guests for any extended amount of time, it wasn't busy and those that came to stay never stayed long, just the way I liked it. Some didn't even bother staying the night when they saw the inn was woman owned. Good riddance.

Had I known how different things were in Somerset, I might've picked another kingdom to run off to. The one thing Somerset had going for it was that no one paid too much attention to me or asked too many questions.

I had managed to keep a low profile, but I should've known my luck was going to run out.

What I didn't expect was that my peace would be shattered so abruptly.

CHAPTER TWO

I glared at Char as he strode in with a grin. His rumpled clothes made his unruly black hair look almost neat. He usually took more care with his appearance, but today he couldn't be bothered. He was too excited to care. He was as happy as I was annoyed. He had a bundle of parchment tucked under his arm and was whistling to himself. *Gods damned ledger day.*

It was far too early for this.

"What are you so happy about?" I asked, not bothering to hide my glare.

He chuckled. "Obviously thrilled to spend time with you," he said, grinning. He danced behind the counter, throwing his arms around me from behind, and quickly planted a kiss on my cheek before I could bat him away.

I groaned. "I hate ledger day."

He laughed again. "You hate most things."

He wasn't wrong, but I felt a grin pull at my lips before I could stop it. His own grin widened more than I thought possible.

"We'll make this quick and painless."

He always said that, but he was very rarely right. It wasn't that the Inn was doing badly, but Char had a head for figures that I certainly didn't. To him, budgeting and planning how to run the Inn was a fun little project. The figures seemed to be a puzzle just waiting for him to crack them. To me, they might as well have been another language.

I had inherited Char when I took over the Rose Lily. I had tried to suggest he didn't need to come by to help anymore, but he dismissed the idea immediately. I tried to be annoyed by that, by him inserting himself into my business, but he had a charm about him that wouldn't let anyone stay upset with him for long. He easily won me over.

In the early days, it was fun having someone around to bounce ideas off. Someone to give suggestions and opinions about how I wanted to change the place. It was good to have someone to talk to.

After Alanna, and then Zara, having him was the only thing that kept me sane. Well, him and Coal, the black cat that had sidled in and made himself at home here after Zara's death.

Coal was named after Char, whose given name was Charcoal, which was a bit of an odd name, but made sense for the son of a pair of herbalists.

Char had been indignant when I named him, not liking the comparison, but since they had both barged into my life and refused to leave, I felt it was apt. Besides, I had reminded him, he wasn't even using the latter half of his name and it was a perfectly good name for a black cat. He had scowled, but after a while him and Coal warmed up to each other. They both took their self-appointed jobs of watching out for me quite seriously.

After Zara, when I was in a dark place, I had tried to push both of them away, but neither of them let me and I was grateful for it.

Char was my best friend and the only person in Somerset I trusted. With the exception of maybe his family. His mother and father ran an apothecary shop that he helped out in when he wasn't here. The few times I had met his family, they seemed incredibly sweet. I enjoyed the visits, but started making excuses not to visit him there when it got to be too much. I missed my own family dearly and their kindness was too much.

His mother especially was incredibly caring. She had privately thanked me for keeping Char occupied, confiding in me that while she loved her son and was grateful he wanted to help around the shop, she sometimes couldn't afford it and needed to get him out from underfoot. He wasn't the most graceful person and more often than not, the vials he was using would break or the salves he was helping mix wouldn't produce the desired effects.

She asked me not to tell him, and I hadn't. There wasn't much breakable in the Inn, and most days I enjoyed his company. Except for the monthly ledger day. Ledger day was the only day I loathed seeing his sunny smile.

After a couple of hours of staring at figures, my head was swimming.

"Haven't we done enough?" I groaned.

He chuckled. "Come on, we're almost done. Hang in there, Del."

"But we've been at it forever," I whined, pulling the sheets closer to me to take another look at what he was working on.

"Hey!" he exclaimed, trying to grasp it back, but he wasn't quick enough to stop me from seeing the name he had been doodling in hearts.

"Ooooh, who's Finley?"

He actually blushed, his face flushing the same crimson of his shirt. "He's no one. Give me that," he said, making another grab for it.

At that moment, Coal jumped up on the table with a loud meow, grabbed the paper in his mouth, and ran off with it.

We stared after his retreating form, dumbstruck, listening to the pitter patter of his paws as he ran down the hallway.

When we both turned back from watching him, we burst into laughter.

"That little menace," he said, chuckling.

"Now you know how I feel; never a moment of peace around here." I said through laughter.

It turned out Coal's intervention was a blessing since it got Char to shorten ledger day, spending most of the rest of the time he could spare trying to catch Coal and get his parchment back.

When it was safely recovered and he had taken his leave, I went back to my desk to get started on the rest of my work. It wasn't lost on me that he had rushed out so quickly to avoid me asking about Finley again. Unfortunately for him, I didn't let things go that easily, but he was lucky I didn't know much of the town.

I kept to myself a lot of the time, so I had no idea who Finley could be. I was almost sure Char had never mentioned him before, though. I would have remembered.

I was still lost in thought when the bell above the door chimed again, startling me out of my thoughts.

I looked to the door for Char. "Forget something?" I asked, but lost my voice when I saw it wasn't him.

It was a woman. Her dark hair fell around her face and down her shoulders in gentle waves. Her bodice did nothing to hide her curves. I struggled to push my eyes to her face. I saw her dark eyes widen in surprise as she took me in. A slight flush appeared on pale cheeks and for the first time in a long time, I felt the curse begin to stir.

I watched as her long lashes fluttered closed for just a moment before she opened them again, and with a tentative smile moved toward me.

Watching her, I couldn't think straight.

A hint of jasmine, or maybe lilies, came wafting in with her. She smiled wider, and my heart stopped. I was instantly drawn to her. Yes, she was beautiful, but it was more than that. There was something about her that pulled me in. I wanted to be close to her, get to know her. I felt the thoughts warring in my mind; she needed to leave immediately, but I couldn't let her go.

She was in danger.

I wanted to scream at her to run. Leave now while you have the chance. Get away from me before I ruin you.

I fought hard to make any of that come out of my mouth, to alter the smile on my face, but I couldn't. As my stare lingered on her, I couldn't stop myself from saying, "What brings a beautiful girl like you to a place like this?"

Her laugh was music to my ears. There wasn't a thing I wouldn't do to hear that laugh again. I could listen to it for the rest of my life. I tried to clear my thoughts. She didn't deserve anything about this.

There was still time to get her to leave, but even the rational part of me was struggling. I wanted to get to know her, to learn anything and everything I could about her.

She faltered a moment when she saw my smile, seeming to sense something was off.

"Just travelling," she said with a shrug. "I needed a change of scenery, and this seemed as nice a place as any." She put down a large pouch on the counter weighed down with silver.

I felt my eyebrows raise. "Will you be staying long?"

She shrugged. "Maybe, maybe not." I continued to look at her, so she added, "I'll probably stay however long it takes the townspeople to run me out with pitchforks."

I laughed, and so did she.

I was a little taller than her, but despite that, I felt quite small, powerless, in her presence. I wasn't one to think often of my appearance, but I wished desperately I had done more to tame my sapphire curls this morning. As they were, they were unruly and wild, not unlike me.

Others spoke of my beauty. After all, I was the beautiful siren who lured guests to my Inn. The rumors used to bother me, but after a time, it became easier to embrace them.

Easier to shroud myself in mystery and false truths then fight them and risk people finding out the truth. Now the rumors gave me some amusement but it still discomforted me how close to the truth people were. I might not be a siren, but I was a monster.

I didn't doubt that I was beautiful in others' eyes, but my own beauty paled in comparison to hers.

I was mesmerized by her dark eyes framed by those sinfully long lashes. She could ask me to do anything, and I would. I had known her all of a few minutes and was already under her spell. I didn't even know her name. I wanted to blame the curse, but I knew this was different. This was me.

The curse had never forced any sort of feelings this strong on me before. It only encouraged the feelings and attraction that were there. It was clear there was something about her, and whatever it was, was dangerous. Not to me, but to her. She needed to leave immediately, but of course, as luck would have it, she was staying indefinitely. Forever if I could get my hands on her. *No.* I fought the thoughts as they came, fought against the pull of the curse. I had to leave her alone, do what little I could to keep her out of danger. The shorter her stay, the better.

The exact opposite came out of my mouth. "I'm honored you chose the Sapphire Siren Inn for your stay. Please feel free, encouraged really, to stay as long as you like. Hells, stay forever, I wouldn't complain." I said with a laugh.

"Who knows, I just might," she said with a grin.

Her smile would kill me. However this ended, that smile was going to haunt me for the rest of my days.

"Well, since you're staying for however long, I should probably know what to call you."

"Princess-" She paused and blushed a bright red. I paled, rushing to pull to mind an image of Somerset's Princess Stella.

I couldn't recall what the Princess looked like, but everyone knew what the King and Queen looked like. I looked her over for a moment, wondering how the blonde, tan royal family could have a princess so opposite them. Her dark hair contrasted stunningly with her pale skin, but she looked nothing like the rest of the royal family.

Her slight chuckle brought me out of my thoughts. "Please ignore me, an old nickname, dreadful really. I'm no princess. I'm Loralie."

"Delphine, and it suits you. A beautiful name for a beautiful woman. Tell me, princess, what brings you to town?"

She looked uncomfortable for a moment before saying, "To tell you the truth, things ended badly with my ex-boyfriend. The whole thing was a mess, and I just couldn't stand to stay there."

I heard little after her saying ex-boyfriend. So much for her potentially being a problem, I thought, feeling both sad and relieved. "I shouldn't have been surprised. It's the same everywhere I go, really. The town before, it was my ex-girlfriend."

Hope shot through me at that before I could think about the consequences. "Things never go well. I don't know why I keep trying. I should know better than to get involved with anyone, really."

I couldn't help letting myself think there was a chance, though. Yes, I corrected, a chance she would get hurt and broken by me like everyone else has.

It sounded like she had enough baggage for the two of us. There wouldn't even be room for my own problems, and I had plenty. A girl like that wouldn't be able to trust me. The curse would claim her. There wouldn't be any way around it, so nothing could happen. But even if nothing could happen, I was dying to know more about her. I figured it couldn't hurt to keep her talking.

"Quite a heartbreaker, huh? It sounds like you left a trail of broken hearts across all of Somerset; hells maybe all of Zanaria."

She smiled sadly. "Something like that. Although not nearly as far as you supposed. I haven't seen all of the Six Realms. Zanaria's quite large you know."

Of course. It was foolish of me to suppose, but she sounded like a traveler, a wanderer like me. At least, like I used to be. A lost soul knows another when they cross paths.

I was adopted into Altea from the island nation of Santerra when I was just a baby. My parents used to say I washed up on shore just to be their little miracle. They say I floated all the way to them from Santerra, drawn to their want for a child.

It was a fairytale, but I liked hearing it, liked hearing that I was wanted.

They took me in and raised me. Altea was the only home I had known, until Bancroft attacked. When the attacks started, most chose to stay, but some families fled or sent their loved ones away. My parents were worried about me and said they wouldn't waste their little miracle for the world.

They pushed me to run. I didn't want to. I begged them to let me stay or to come away with me, but they were needed in Altea, so I set out on my own.

I went South, away from the northern kingdom of Bancroft to the safety of Somerset. Although safety is a relative term. Had I known what was waiting for me here, I would have taken my chances in Altea.

There wasn't anything I wouldn't do to leave this place. Hells, I would have gone willingly to the King Slayer himself, King Damien of Bancroft. Whatever he would have done to me couldn't have been a worse fate than the curse I met here.

I shook myself from my thoughts and noticed that she too had a faraway look in her eye. She looked like she understood my pain, and I hated that for her. I wanted to draw her back from wherever she went, but before I could think of anything, the curse intervened.

I put my hand to my heart dramatically and said, "Well, do promise you'll go easy on me then, princess."

She smiled at that, but it didn't touch her eyes, and she stayed silent.

"Well, if there's anything at all I can do to make your stay more enjoyable, just let me know. I'm at your service." I couldn't stop myself, and didn't know if I wanted to, from running my eyes up and down her curves before adding, "Really, anything at all." I licked my lips before adding, "It would be my pleasure."

She seemed too distracted to have noticed the cringey, blatant innuendo. She just thanked me, took her key, and went to her room.

Not a moment later, Coal jumped up on the desk and bumped his head into me. I relented to his demands and began petting him.

"She's something, isn't she?"

"Meow."

"I know, right?" I said with a groan. "I totally blew it."

"Meow."

"You don't have to tell me twice." I scratched under his chin, and couldn't help my smile when he started purring loudly. Maybe things here weren't so bad after all.

As long as I could find a way to keep this new girl, Loralie, safe from me, I could continue to live a somewhat normal existence.

Besides, from the impression I made on her, I was sure she wasn't in any danger. It should have been a relief, but it bothered me. Her being distracted and disinterested should have been a huge weight off my chest, but there was something about her and her sad smile that made me determined to get to know her. There was something about her that made me determined to see another genuine smile.

Chapter Three

Contrary to my fears and hopes, I didn't see much of my mysterious, gorgeous guest for a while.

It seemed she had a habit of sleeping well into the afternoon and only emerging from her room when the moon could be seen ascending into the sky.

When she did emerge, she just smiled in greeting, but much to my chagrin, she didn't stop to say hello, just headed out the door without a backward glance.

I should have been happy, but it was hard to stop myself from regretting that she didn't seem to want to get to know me. I had only known her a few days, and I was already missing her when she left. This would end terribly.

I waited and waited for her to come back, well after the time I would have normally gone to sleep. I couldn't bring myself to leave the desk without seeing her back safe. It had been hours, and I didn't know her habits, but it seemed strange.

Coal visited me while I was watching for her, startling me with a loud, "Meow!"

I jumped at the noise before realizing it was him. "Coal, you scared me!"

I moved to pet him, but he sauntered past me and settled on the far end of my desk, watching me.

"I know I'm up later than usual, but the new girl isn't back yet."

"Meow."

"I know I don't have to stay up, but it seems weird she isn't back yet. What if something happened to her?"

"Meow." I swear I could see him raising his non-existent eyebrows at me.

"I know I'm being dramatic. You don't have to tell me twice."

"Meow."

"I'll go to sleep soon, don't worry about me, bud."

With a sharp huff, he jumped off the desk and sauntered away, leaving me feeling a little alone and a whole lot of judgment.

When the door finally opened, revealing her, I could have kicked myself. She wasn't alone. I don't know why I thought any different. Of course she wasn't alone. Holding her hand was a short man who looked to be her age. Well, come to think of it, I didn't actually know how old she was, but they both looked to be in their late twenties. I don't know why I just assumed she was around my age. From the way she looked and acted, she really could have been any age. She had a young-looking face, but a maturity about her that made me almost certain she wasn't as young as she looked. I would have to ask. Later, once she detached herself from the luckiest man in Zanaria.

I watched as she ran her fingers through his hair and laughed at something he had said. I could have killed him. I wouldn't have considered death too steep a price for his crime. He wasn't anywhere near worthy of her. He wasn't fit to be near her, never mind getting that sort of attention from her. I knew I could beat him in a fight, even before the curse, but especially now. All it would take was me wrapping my fingers around his neck and squeezing, squeezing until the struggling stopped and the light left his eyes.

"Oh!" Loralie exclaimed when she noticed me. "I'm so sorry. I didn't expect anyone to still be up."

He whispered something in her ear, and I watched as his lips trailed down, planting kisses on her neck.

Strangling was too good for him, too quick.

She giggled and leaned into him a moment before remembering me. A blush overtook her face, making her complexion match her crimson dress. The neckline plunged far enough that I could see the blush spread down to her chest.

I brought my eyes back to her face and saw her shoo him away from her neck, but not too far away. She still held his hand. She looked like she had been caught sneaking a suitor past her parents.

The last thing I needed was to continue to watch his lips on her neck. I didn't think I could have managed it without violence. Thoughts of choking the life out of him came back. I clearly wasn't subtle about my mood, since she smiled apologetically before leading him up the stairway to her room.

I was stupid to have stayed up. She was a grown woman, and I didn't even know her. I didn't need to look out for her. No one had asked me to, and she clearly didn't care that I had.

I stalked down the hall, up the back stairs to my own room, praying to the gods I wouldn't hear them. Otherwise, I knew I would do something regretful, even if I wouldn't regret it.

Thankfully, the inn was quiet from my room. I finished getting ready for bed and slipped under the covers. Only then did it occur to me how weird it was that I couldn't hear them. She was only staying a couple of rooms down, and she didn't seem like the quiet type. At least they were being courteous to the other guests, I thought ruefully. The last thing I wanted to deal with in the morning, which, by the looks of the lightening sky through my window, was rapidly approaching, was unhappy guests.

Chapter Four

The next day I rose far later than usual, rushed through getting ready, and practically ran to the front desk.

When I got there, the only thing out of place was Coal sitting on my desk. He wasn't normally awake this early, but there he was sitting there judging me. I could feel the appraisal as his furry little face watched me. He blinked slowly at me and I could almost hear him asking if I knew what time it was.

"I'm barely late," I said with an indignant huff.

I moved behind the desk, ready to shoo him off my stack of parchment, but he got up on his own and turned, his tail whacking me in the face before he jumped down.

"Hey!" I exclaimed, but he was already scampering down the hall.

I hadn't meant to oversleep, but I had stayed up far too late last night, clearly for no reason. Coal wasn't wrong; normally I was down checking on the rest of the staff and making sure none of the guests needed anything far earlier than this. Thankfully, nothing had fallen apart in my absence.

On the bright side, Loralie's nighttime guest would have left by now. Maybe it was for the better. I didn't know that I could have calmly dealt with seeing him. The last thing I needed was him winding up dead at my Inn. That would definitely be bad for business.

I sighed, letting myself enjoy the thought of him no longer breathing, before sitting back down and checking my tasks for the day. There was always something that needed doing. Maybe today I would finally get around to fixing the door to the dining room. It probably wouldn't take too long. I considered it for a moment, but it could wait. It would be irresponsible to leave the desk unattended so soon after just opening it for the day. Besides, my book was calling out to me. I settled in, took my book from the desk, and picked up where I left off.

It was a lovely tale about a wordsmith in a strange land. Whoever penned it had a wild imagination, though, with all the talk of dwellings stacked on top of one another so tall they touched the sky. The wordsmith was to be attending a ball, which I had gathered was less commonplace there than it was here. She was meeting up with some of the other ladies attending when I heard footsteps on the stairs.

I stashed the book away quickly and looked up. Loralie's guest was still here. Why was he still here? As I watched, he stumbled his way down the stairs. I hoped he would fall and break his neck, but to my chagrin, he made it down the stairs without incident. He was holding a hand to his head and seemed dazed. It wouldn't be the first or last time a guest indulged too much. I was surprised she hadn't bid him leave earlier, though. Maybe she had overindulged last night as well.

The afternoon faded into evening without her appearing. I was starting to get concerned. I thought about maybe getting her some water and a hangover draught. I twisted the idea around in my head, but it seemed too forward, so I fought to keep myself at the desk.

Coal sauntered over, so I leaned down to pet him only for him to sidestep me. He turned to look at me and I could see the judgment in his eyes. Even Coal knew how ridiculous I was being about Loralie. I sighed and tried to focus my mind on my duties, but that didn't work. I tried reading but couldn't stop thinking about her. I knew I was going to cave.

I threw down my book in frustration and heard a laugh. "That bad, huh?"

I looked up quickly, knowing even before I did, that it was her. When I looked up, I saw her standing in front of me in another crimson number that, if possible, looked even better on her than the one yesterday.

I just stared at her. How could I not? Seconds passed, but it could have been minutes. I had lost the power of speech. Her onyx hair cascaded over her shoulders and down her back in loose waves. I wanted to step closer and run my fingers through her hair. I wondered if it was as smooth and silky as it looked. I heard a noise come from her lips, drawing my eyes to them. I wondered if they were as soft as they looked. A moment later, it occurred to me she was speaking and that I should be mortified. I was just standing there, staring at her. I might as well have been drooling.

She paused and must have seen in my face I hadn't heard what she was saying. She laughed before saying again, "Clearly, I need to read that book immediately if it's gotten you that out of it. I've been meaning to pick up something new to read."

"I haven't read much of it yet, but you can borrow it if you'd like."

"I wouldn't dare leave you in suspense like that, but the moment you finish it, I'd love to borrow it."

I hadn't read much of the story, so I hoped it was one good enough to recommend. I couldn't tell her the truth; that I hadn't even remotely been thinking about the book.

Coal suddenly launched himself on the desk in front of me, announcing his presence with a loud, "Meow."

If I wasn't so used to him, it would have startled me. I hadn't seen him coming. Loralie smiled widely at him. "Who's this?" she asked.

"His name's Coal." She started to reach out a hand toward him and I quickly added, "He's not the friendliest. I wouldn't-" But she already had her hand in front of him. I winced as he moved his head closer to her, waiting for the teeth or claws to come out.

He wasn't usually friendly with the guests, preferring to stay out of sight, and didn't like to be approached by them. Even with Char, it took a good few months for Coal to warm up to him.

My jaw dropped when Coal licked her hand. She giggled as his tongue brushed against her, and when he stopped, he bumped his head against her hand and let her pet him.

To my continued amazement, he started purring loudly at her touch and after a few pets, rolled over and showed his belly to her.

"Careful," I cautioned. When he did that, he was just as likely to claw and attack you as he was to let you pet him. "It might be a trap-" I started to explain, but she was already petting him, making cooing noises, and his purrs had increased.

After a couple more minutes, something caught his attention and he flipped over, jumped off the desk, and bounded down the hall.

We both watched him go, and when she turned back to me, I told her, "He's not normally that friendly."

She grinned. "He's such a sweetie. I'm so glad I'll be staying a while."

Conflicted about her staying a while, unsure if I wanted to encourage or discourage her, I struggled for something else to talk about. I glanced down at the desk and my book laying there reminded me she had been excited about the books, so I rushed to tell her, "You know, if you're looking for something before then, we do have a library here."

Her eyes lit up and a smile stole over her face, making me wish I had brought it up earlier. "You do?" she asked.

I grinned back. Her excitement was contagious. "It's not as big as I'd like, but we have over a thousand books, so hopefully something will be to your taste."

Her jaw dropped as she looked at me with a mix of wonder and shock. "A thousand books?"

I nodded.

"Which way?" she asked.

I pointed down the hall, and she ran that way, before screeching to a halt when she realized all the hallway doors were closed and she didn't know where she was going. I laughed, but before she could ask, I yelled over, "On your left."

She pivoted and saw the door, stopping for a moment in front of it and taking a deep breath before opening it. I heard her shriek from down the hall and couldn't help laughing. A few minutes later, she came back, a little sheepishly, holding a book tightly to her chest. I strained to see which one but couldn't see the title.

"Would it be okay if I take this upstairs to read tonight?" she asked with a pleading in her voice that I knew I wouldn't say no to, even if it had been against the rules. It wasn't, though. Guests were encouraged to enjoy the library at their leisure.

I nodded and told her, "Of course. You're more than welcome to take as many as you like to your room."

Her eyes lit up when she smiled. She looked wistfully over her shoulder in the direction of the library. "I would love to, but I don't have the time to pick out any. I have to head out." She looked down, remembered the book in her hand, and added, "But first I have to run this upstairs."

"I can take that up-" I started to say, but she had already taken off back up the stairs. She moved more quickly than I would have imagined possible. A minute or so later, she returned, running down the stairs. I thought she was going to leave the Inn just as quickly, but my heart fluttered when she skidded to a stop in front of the desk. "Thank you," she said with a smile. "If it isn't too much trouble, do you think you could help me pick out some books for the rest of my stay?"

I jumped at the thought, literally. I was out of my chair in an instant, smiling widely. "I'd love to. Why don't we go look-"

She frowned. "I'm so sorry. I should have been clearer. I meant tomorrow." She, again, looked wistfully at the library and then sadly at me. I wondered for a moment if she regretted not being able to spend time with me, but that wouldn't make sense. She didn't even really know me. "I wish I could tonight, but I have an evening engagement."

I hoped it wasn't like her evening engagement yesterday, I thought, fighting to keep a scowl from my face. I nodded while attempting a smile. "Very well then, tomorrow it is."

"It's a date," she said with a grin, before turning and heading out quickly. "Don't wait up," she added with a chuckle.

I hadn't been planning to, but I couldn't sleep. I kept replaying our conversation over and over in my mind. I needed to know what she meant when she said it was a date. She couldn't have actually meant a date. If she did, I shouldn't do it. Every inch of me was screaming to be close to her after only a couple of days, but then again, she clearly didn't feel the same, so maybe it was okay. After all, she had brought a man back to her room the night before. Just thinking about it made me want to hit something, strangle someone, specifically the man in question, but that had to be a pretty clear indicator she wasn't interested in me.

I desperately wanted to spend time with her, and she was only in danger if she caught any sort of feelings. She hadn't, and I reasoned she wouldn't. Not for me; not when she looked like that, and I looked like me. Not that there was anything wrong with the way I looked. I was a little taller than her and when I managed to tame my unruly sapphire hair, I thought I might pass for pretty. My nose was a little large for my face, my ears weren't quite as rounded as I thought they ought to be, and my face was rather angular, but the townsfolk spoke of my beauty so there must be something to it.

In my own right, I was sure I did possess some beauty, but standing next to Loralie, I didn't think it was possible for anyone to feel beautiful.

For the first time since the curse struck, I found myself longing for a mirror, wondering how the time had changed me and what I might look like to her, but it was foolish of me.

Even if there were mirrors to be found anywhere besides Room 13, I wouldn't risk it. I hadn't looked in a mirror since my hair turned the sapphire it was now, since the curse happened. I broke every mirror in the place after that day. I tried to start with the mirror in Room 13, the most offensive of the mirrors, but it was the only one that wouldn't break.

I took my frustration out on all the other mirrors. I was scared of what I might see, of what might happen if I used a mirror again. As it was, I hadn't seen my own reflection clearly since the curse happened, so I had to imagine what she saw when she looked at me, and I wasn't imagining a pretty picture.

I had to be safe spending time with her. Besides, she seemed okay with the idea, too. She had asked me to help her. What kind of innkeeper would I be if I didn't indulge my guests' requests?

"Ehh hmhm." I startled violently, looking up to see a guest standing in front of the desk.

I waited for him to say something, but he didn't, just stared at me, waiting. After a moment of silence, I asked, "Yes?"

He looked offended, puffing up his chest before saying, "Well, since you so politely asked how you could help me, we're out of towels, room 4. Bring some up."

He stormed off, but not quickly enough. Lucky for him, I had a stack of towels under the desk. Unlucky for him, I had good aim. I whipped two rolled-up towels at the back of his head, one after another. Both were direct hits. He stopped in his tracks before turning slowly, looking outraged.

I held in my laughter as best I could and smiled sweetly at him. "I found your towels and made sure to deliver them with haste."

He looked at me in disbelief before scooping up the towels, muttering to himself about the treatment here and how he'd certainly be telling his friends about it. Good. The last thing I wanted was more people like him staying here.

Nights like this, after encountering guests like him, I couldn't help but feel more homesick than usual. I missed Altea and my family. I missed how even strangers were kind there. The people of Somerset were judgmental and mistrusted me. It wasn't that I liked most of them either, and of course, it got worse after the curse, but even before the people were wary of foreigners.

They also didn't seem to know what to do with a strong-willed woman. My owning and running the Inn gave most of them pause. Sometimes I wondered if that would have been enough on its own to turn the town against me without the curse. It hardly mattered though, when my hair turned sapphire and my behavior became wild, most of the town believed I had gone mad.

Well, everyone except for Char. There was no getting rid of him and while he sometimes drove me crazy, I was grateful for him. I owned my remaining sanity to him as the only true friend I had in this whole kingdom. I found myself wondering what he might think of Loralie before chasing the thought from my mind. I picked up my book to try to force my thoughts onto anything else, knowing even as I was picking it up that it wouldn't work.

Chapter Five

I stayed at the desk for another hour attempting to read before deciding it was hopeless and abandoning the book. I was frustrated. Loralie hadn't returned yet, and I knew I shouldn't be up waiting for her, but I couldn't bring myself to leave and knew I wouldn't sleep even if I did.

At least Coal was keeping me company, curled up on a corner on my desk. I occupied my time petting Coal and thinking about what books Loralie might like and what I could recommend to her. It would have helped if I had seen what she took up to her room earlier, but the longer it took to find suggestions and recommendations, the longer I got to spend with her. I was quite alright with that.

Another hour passed, and even Coal had abandoned the desk. He was probably lounging by the fire or curled up in my bed. I decided he had the right idea; it was way past time to call it a night.

She might be out all night, who knows, but I didn't need to wait any longer. I put away my things for the night and made my way up to my room.

I was turning my door handle when I heard laughter that was unmistakably hers, and from the sounds on the stairs, it didn't sound like she was alone. I opened my door quickly, not wanting a repeat of yesterday, not sure I could keep my cool seeing him with her again, knowing she picked him to spend the night with her again. I didn't want to see.

I went to close the door behind me and heard her musical laughter again, this time closer. I couldn't help myself. I left the door open a crack and stuck my head out. It turns out I didn't need to be that careful; they were so wrapped up in each other neither of them noticed me.

The anger spiked through me but was quickly replaced by shock when I looked at the man. He was taller and stockier than the man from yesterday. I pulled my head back into my room, pushing the door shut, not caring to stifle the noise.

I couldn't decide whether it was better or worse that it wasn't the same man. She wasn't letting him enjoy the paradise of a second night with her. But where was she finding these men? What was so special about either of them? What did they have that I didn't? My last thought before I drifted off to sleep was that the only thing they had that I didn't was her attention. It was for the best really, with the curse, I knew I wasn't safe for her, but that didn't lessen the sting of rejection or the depth of my longing. What I wouldn't have given to have her look at me like that.

CHAPTER SIX

When her latest conquest came stumbling down the stairs the next morning, clutching his head like his predecessor, I made sure to loudly tell him to, "Have a great rest of your afternoon!" on the way out.

He clutched his head harder, making me laugh when he shut the door.

That helped a little to quiet the rage in me. I had no right to be feeling this way. She was her own person, and there was no reason she shouldn't be able to have fun with whoever she wanted, but I hated the thought of anyone getting to touch her. I wanted to run my fingers through her hair and pull her in close. I would kill for just a kiss, literally.

If I thought murdering either of those men would make her look in my direction, I probably would have done it.

Whatever she was doing with them, I hoped she was happy. I knew they were from how dazed they left the next morning. Whatever she was doing to them, I wanted nothing more than to experience it myself.

I hoped she would, at the very least, remember our talk from yesterday and still want to look at the library with me. I had been spending most of the morning, and a lot of last night, coming up with book recommendations for her.

I wanted to spend time with her. The curse was pushing me to pursue her faster and harder than I wanted, but the truth remained, I wanted her. Curse or no curse, I would have been trying to get her attention. But I was cursed, and I had to be mindful of that. I couldn't slip up like I did last time. I couldn't lose another person I cared about, especially not to my own hands.

After Zara, it had taken me weeks to be able to look myself in the mirror. I didn't want to face myself and know I was looking at a killer. I couldn't stomach it. Alanna's death had been in a fit of passion, but Zara's death was more calculated and even more devastating. She hadn't done a damn thing wrong besides meeting me, and now I had to live with the fact that she was dead, and I was to blame. There were no excuses, no one to pin the blame on or hide behind. It was my fault.

Sometimes when I closed my eyes, I could still see the life leaving hers. I could still feel my mind screaming at me to stop. I fought as hard as I could, but I couldn't control myself. I watched, internally screaming, as my own hands strangled the life out of her. The curse took control, only letting me stop after she stopped breathing.

I started compressions the moment I regained control. I could barely see her through my tears, but I had to save her. I tried to breathe air back into her lungs. I screamed and pleaded to every deity I knew the name of, but she was already gone.

I sobbed for the rest of the day over her lifeless body. I hadn't truly realized the horror of the curse until then. I hadn't really understood what it would mean. I had thought it would be easy to get around. If she just didn't open the door, she would be safe. If she cared about me, she would have listened when I warned her, but she hadn't.

She gave into temptation, for whatever reason I'll never know.

In the early days of the curse, I had thought I would feel betrayed by anyone that entered. I had thought that if I was forced to entrust someone with the key and they ignored my warnings and went inside anyway, I would feel betrayed enough that I would have wanted to kill them.

I wished I had felt that way with Zara. It would've been easier if I had felt anything but devastation. I hated myself and still did. I wasn't worthy of being loved by anyone.

Alanna had been the first to show me that. She had only been with me for my connections. She continually asked me about my life in Altea, about the royals and my family. My parents were close advisors to the Queens. The joke was on her, though. I hadn't had any contact with my family or anyone else in Altea since I ran. I had tried in the beginning, but none of the messages I sent were ever answered. It had to be because of the shield. No one got in or out of Altea now, but that meant the King hadn't breached the shield either, meaning thank the gods, everyone was safe, for now.

When I left, I travelled blindly from town to town, unsure what I was looking for but sure I had to make it further from Altea and from Bancroft, but not wanting to stray too far from the only home, the only family I had ever known.

I travelled as far as I could, to this forgotten corner of Somerset, took a room at the Inn, and fell in love with the peace and quiet.

For the first time since I left home, the sorrow in my heart quieted. I wasn't about to take that for granted. It may have been impulsive, but I gave every last coin and bought the place. Back then, I thought to stay until things were safe and then sell the place to the first person who offered when it was safe to return home. It was laughable now, really. My haven, my sanctuary, had become my prison.

A part of me still loved the Inn for the peace it had given me back then. I didn't regret buying it, until

Alanna and the curse.

Things got worse after Zara died. I lost my will to live. At my lowest, I tried to end things, only to find the curse wouldn't let go of me. Char found me and the pain in his eyes was enough to ensure I didn't try again. I could deal with my own pain well enough, but the idea of inflicting pain on him was unbearable.

The incident was good for one thing, though, it taught me that the curse kept me trapped in more ways than one. Not only was I essentially tied to the Inn, but I was tied to life, or, at the very least, couldn't end my life with my own hands.

Char didn't know what to do with me, which was around the time that Coal showed up. He sauntered into the Inn and into my life, making himself right at home. Without those two I would be lost. That was the first time Char lent me a book. He was out of ideas for how to help and lent me his favorite story.

I was enraptured by the vivid imagery of the far-off places and the romance. I drank down every word and surfaced begging for more. I hadn't paid much attention to the library before then, but after it became my favorite room.

I found that burying myself in stories helped to bury some of my grief, despair, and loneliness. I was grateful for that small mercy.

After a while, it occurred to me to try to research the curse, but I couldn't find any reference to or mention of it.

I still hadn't been able to find a thing on it. It was useless. I was beyond saving and was content to stay away from everyone, with the exception of Char, of course, ... until Loralie walked in.

There was something about her I just couldn't stay away from. The curse was part of it, but even in my own thoughts, I wanted to be close to her. I needed to get her to leave. I should have felt ashamed of myself for considering spending the day looking at books with her.

There was no way that was even remotely acceptable. The more time I spent around her, the more I craved her. At this rate, I would be forced to give her the key by tomorrow. I couldn't let that happen. I had no idea things would move this fast, that my own feelings would progress this quickly. With Zara it had taken a couple of weeks for me to start feeling like this, and a couple more for me to have to give her the key, and that was only after we had slept together. I hadn't even kissed Loralie, and I could already feel the compulsion.

I knew it would be smart to avoid her, but I couldn't bring myself to. I could hardly think about anything besides her.

When she finally emerged, I knew it was her before I even looked up. I could hear her light footsteps and smell her jasmine perfume. I fought to keep my eyes on my work, wondering if she wouldn't engage with me if I didn't look up, but I heard her approach. My head and eyes raised of their own accord. She was wearing an oversized wool sweater and tights and was holding a book tightly to her chest.

She smiled at me and said, "I know you said to help myself, but I was hoping I could take you up on your offer to show me around the library."

Gods be damned. I couldn't say no to her. I raised an eyebrow at her, not able to resist teasing her. "You mean show you around the single room I overgenerously call a library?"

She laughed at that, her neck turning red as she blushed a little. I wanted to run my tongue up her neck and whisper in her ear about some other things we could do instead of exploring the library.

Before I could say or do anything besides stare at her, she explained, "I didn't mean show me around. I meant your offer from yesterday. I'm not sure what I should read next."

I wondered if I could make her blush deepen. I smiled and said, "If you wanted to get me alone, you could have just said that." I couldn't help throwing in a wink.

She laughed before saying, "You're quite stunning, but I really would like to see your collection and get some recommendations. I finished my story last night and don't know what to read next. I assume you're not done with yours?"

Reeling from her calling me stunning, it took me a long moment to process the rest of what she said. I looked down at the abandoned book in my desk. I hadn't touched it since yesterday and hadn't been able to read much then either. I hadn't been able to focus on much of anything lately with her under the same roof. A moment later, it occurred to me to be surprised that she had somehow found time to finish the book between when she came back with her nighttime guest and now. It couldn't have been more than a couple of hours since he left. That was impressive, even for me, and I normally read fast.

At least I did before she showed up. I couldn't stop the thoughts of her, of what I would love to do with and to her, and of what she might be doing when she wasn't standing in front of me. I'd never experienced anything like this before with anyone else. Even with Zara, she had never invaded nearly my every waking thought like Loralie had.

I smiled at her. "Well, I'd love to give recommendations, but first, what book did you just finish?"

She gestured to the book with her free hand. "This one."

"Which is called?"

She blushed again, which told me all I needed to know, even before she said, "It's not important."

"Well, it is if you want good recommendations."

She shook her head. "Never mind. I'll just look myself."

"Come on. It can't be that bad. Just tell me."

She shook her head again. I went to move from behind the desk, but she took off toward the library. Laughing, I gave chase, slowing my pace to let her win.

I heard her laughing as I entered the library. She yelled triumphantly as she shoved the book back into its place. I noted the location so I could look later, but right now that wasn't what I had on my mind. I moved quickly, coming up behind her. She whirled around and jumped back in surprise when she saw I was much closer than she expected. She had her back pressed against the bookcase now. I leaned one of my arms over her head on the bookshelf behind her and watched her.

Her cheeks flushed. I loved how she reacted to me. She was breathless, but managed to say, "I win."

I watched her, bringing my other hand up to her shoulder and tracing my finger down her arm.

"You mean you don't think I know the book is behind you?"

She paled for a moment, before straightening as much as she could and saying, "You can't possibly know which of the many books near us is the one I just put back."

"Oh, but I do."

She didn't seem to believe me. She smiled. "You're all talk."

"Not quite. I just love seeing you squirm."

"Well, it's not working. You won't win. You're not seeing the book."

"I think we both know you're wrong."

"Prove it."

"I easily could." I let my fingers move from her arm, up to her neck, lazily tracing a trail of where I couldn't stop thinking about putting my lips. "But I might not look. I wouldn't want to offend your sensibilities as a lady."

"I'm no lady."

"You seem terribly proper, princess." I said with a smirk. "Are you worried someone might find out what you read?"

"No," she said defiantly.

"Well, I think you are." I started to move my hand to where I knew the book was, taunting her. "I think you're quite worried I might see that you-"

She cut me off, and caught me off-guard, spinning me so my back was against the bookshelf.

"Wow. Someone's feisty. If I had known you liked to be in charge-"

She cut me off with her lips, stopping every thought in my brain. She ran her tongue over my bottom lip before biting down and I felt the warmth of my blood before her tongue captured it. I hadn't in my wildest dreams thought she would take charge like this, be rough like this. No wonder those men left so dazed. I couldn't have told you my own name. Nothing existed outside of her. For once, my mind was quiet.

Until she pulled away and the horror of what happened hit me. The curse. My fingers were already itching toward the pocket I knew the key was in. I couldn't let that happen. I felt like panicking, but, thankfully, the curse kicked in enough to force me into some semblance of calm. At least until I saw her face. She looked how I felt. Fuck. As much as that couldn't happen again, I had foolishly hoped she would want it to.

"Wow," I said.

"I'm so sorry!" she blurted out. "I don't know what came over me, but I promise you it won't happen again."

I was stunned and, for once, me and the curse were at a loss for words. She bolted from the room before I could think of anything to say.

I didn't see her for the rest of the day, but when I went back to the library to see what she had been reading, the book and several others were missing. In the place of the book I had been looking for was a single lily. She couldn't have left it for me, couldn't have meant it for me, not after that reaction, but I took it anyway. I put it on my nightstand, unable to resist. It smelled like her.

CHAPTER SEVEN

When Char came to visit the next day, he immediately noticed something different about me and was quick to ask, "What's got you looking like that?"

I was surprised, but I shouldn't have been. Char was good at reading me.

"There might be a girl," I started.

But he cut me off with a loud, "Gods, tell me everything!" His goofy grin was adorable and I hated that I couldn't smile with him.

I hated that he didn't know what was holding me back. He had been encouraging me since Zara "left" to start dating again. He knew I was a mess when she "left", but that was all I could tell him. The curse wouldn't allow me to tell anyone.

"It's not like that. Well, I mean it sort of is, or I wanted it to be, but she's not into me like that."

He looked at me skeptically. "What makes you say that?"

"Well, she quite literally ran screaming from me."

He chuckled at that. "She did not. What actually happened?"

I just blinked at him, and after a moment his face fell. "No, really. What happened?"

I let the silence continue longer and he looked crestfallen for me. "I'm so sorry."

"It's stupid. I came on too strong when she had been giving me signals the whole time that she's not into me like that. I was so stupid. Gods, she brings a new man here pretty much every night. She's not interested in me."

He watched me a few moments longer. I wished I could tell him more, explain to him why it was for the best, but I had long since given up trying to evade the curse.

"Well, it's her loss then, but I'm so excited you're finally ready to put yourself back out there! It's been far too long for you to be alone. I happen to know a couple of eligible ladies that would be happy to be courted by you."

I didn't know if it was true or not, but I wasn't in the mood. Even though Loralie had made it clear how she felt, she was still the only one in my thoughts. Besides, the last thing I wanted was to drag other ladies into danger, but Char didn't give up easily. In a moment of brilliance, I thought of the perfect deal.

"Tell you what, as soon as you invite Finley out for a meal, I'll meet one of your eligible ladies."

He groaned. "That's so not fair! This is not even remotely the same thing. Finley's no one."

"Well, that's too bad then. Maybe your eligible ladies can court each other."

He sighed and slung his arm around my shoulder. "Just me and you together forever then, huh?"

I couldn't help laughing with him, but in truth it didn't sound bad to me. At least I knew he was safe and there were certainly worse people to spend time with.

He stayed most of the day, but luckily, I was able to usher him out before Loralie made an appearance.

Not that I saw much of her either. I only caught a glimpse of her coming down the stairs in a hurry before she rushed out the door. It almost felt like she was running from me. She was smart to stay away from me, but it killed me inside to see her almost seem afraid of me. I had no idea what I had done or what she had seen that would have made her feel like that, but it was for the best. If I didn't have to spend more time with her, she would be safe, protected. But I couldn't bring myself to be anything but miserable about it.

She went out wearing another barely-there dress, and by now I knew the drill. I knew I should go to bed before she returned. The last thing I wanted was to see her with anyone else. The last thing I needed was to rip out some guy's throat in the middle of the entryway because she preferred him. That would hardly help my case and would just push her further from me.

I was going to go to bed until I saw the flower on my nightstand where I had left it. It was just a silly little lily; it didn't mean anything. It couldn't mean anything after how she had acted, after how she ran out on me, but I couldn't help hoping.

Against my better judgment, I put the lily behind my ear and without bothering to change, threw on my silk robe and descended the stairs. I couldn't decide if it was my idea or if it was another oh-so-subtle push from the curse, but I found myself waiting at my desk in the entryway for her.

Coal stopped by a few times, meowing at me to go back to bed. He was probably right, but to his dismay, I continued to wait.

I wasn't surprised when, in the middle of the night, she showed up with another new guy. I watched as she smiled at him, wanting to make him suffer for having done nothing to earn her smiles, for not appreciating what a gift they were.

Her smile faded when she saw me. I watched her eyes travel up the silk of my robe and shivered under her gaze. I was absolutely making a fool of myself, but I couldn't help but get some satisfaction out of the way she was looking at me. She pulled her hand out of his and whispered something to him. He went up the stairs, leaving us alone.

She didn't say anything, just continued to stare at me. The hunger in her eyes was a clear invitation. I sidled up closer to her and reached out my hand tentatively. When she didn't move, I let myself run my fingers through her hair, pulling her closer to me, caressing her beautifully soft raven hair. I was surprised she let me. She didn't bat my hand away, move back, or even tell me to stop. She actually leaned into my touch. When she met my eye, she looked surprised by her own actions and blushed. The blood rushing to her pale cheeks and the way she looked at me did me in. I melted.

She was the first person in a long time to look at me like that. She would be different. She had to be, because I couldn't let her go. The curse would always hang over my head, but she could be the one to stop it. It couldn't be broken, but as long as she didn't break my trust, the curse could be stopped. If she stayed, as long as she was here and the curse was attached to her, I could be free.

I saw our future flash before my eyes. Us sitting by the fire cuddled up together reading. Us holding hands and taking a moonlight stroll through the gardens. Us doing whatever it was she did with those men that left them so dazed leaving her room. I could see it all. Maybe she would be the one to save me.

I didn't say any of that. I just smiled down at her and told her, "If there's anything at all I can do to make your stay more," I licked my lips, "*enjoyable,* just let me know." I let my hand stroke down her hair to her face, and lifted her chin, moving her eyes to mine. "Just say the word. I'm all yours."

Her blush and the look in her eyes told me she understood my meaning and would be thinking about it tonight. *Good.* I sauntered back to the desk, swinging my hips more exaggeratedly than usual. I couldn't help looking back, and when I saw her watching, I winked before tossing my cobalt hair over my shoulder and closed the distance to the desk. There was nothing I could do to stop her if she continued to take men to her bed, but from the hunger in her eyes when I saw her watching me, I was sure she would be thinking about me.

Chapter Eight

I rose with a new purpose and a new hope the next day. I was going to make her notice me. Curse be damned, I wanted her. I couldn't bear to think of her not being in my life, especially when she seemed interested, at least physically. I was sure if she would give me a chance that she would see there was something between us. This couldn't possibly be one sided. I had to get her attention, and I had just the plan.

I rushed through my daily tasks that morning, making sure to give myself plenty of time in the kitchen. I pulled on an apron and got to work.

Coal showed up to supervise of course. I was impressed I only had to shoo him off the counter a couple of times. Normally, he was a much bigger distraction, but the second time he bumped into one of the flour cannisters, sending it and himself off the counter. He scampered off with his newfound white spots, his tail trailing flour in his wake.

An hour or so later, I finished drizzling the icing on and took off the apron with a satisfied sigh. There wasn't much I felt like I could do right in my life, especially now, but no one made a better cinnamon roll than I did.

The scent of cinnamon wafted through the kitchen, and I couldn't help myself from having one. There were plenty anyway. I sunk my teeth into one with a satisfied groan. It had been far too long since I'd last baked anything, too long since I felt okay doing anything that might bring me any sort of joy. But I wanted to get to know Loralie, and what better ice breaker than my cinnamon rolls?

I used to make them all the time, back before the curse. The guests used to love them. I would make them fresh every morning, but I hadn't since that day. I couldn't stomach the thought. Just the smell of cinnamon used to bring me right back there. I was pleasantly surprised it didn't anymore. Pleasantly surprised I could let myself feel happy, feel some joy, without feeling too guilty about it.

I put a few cinnamon rolls into a basket and made the trek upstairs, willing myself not to think about how similar this felt to that day. It was a true feat of strength that I made it past room 13 without looking at the door.

A few doors later and I was at hers. I had written a little note that I attached to the basket since I didn't want to disturb her. I figured she might still be sleeping, based on her nighttime habits.

I put the basket outside her door, and stood there, unsure if I should knock. After a minute of wavering, I decided to knock gently. If she was sleeping, I wouldn't disturb her, but if she was awake, at least she would know someone had been there and left something for her.

I tapped gently on the door for a moment before turning and going back the way I came. I was halfway down the hall when I heard a door open. "Hello?"

I turned around and saw Loralie poking her head out of her door. Her hair was a mess of tangles and snarls and she didn't look pleased to be woken up, but she looked adorable. I stifled a giggle and waved sheepishly. "Morning, princess." She scowled, and I laughed. "Well, I should say Good Afternoon."

She grumbled and went to shut the door before seeing the basket. "What's this?"

I watched as she picked them up and tried not to blush as she read the note. Her eyes widened. She peeled back the cloth over the basket and gasped. "You made these?" She looked up at me with wide eyes. "For me?"

I smiled and shrugged. "I figured we had gotten off to a weird start, and I wanted to apologize for that. I would love to get to know you if you'd give me that chance." It was rare when the curse let me truly speak from the heart like I was now, rare for my wants to align with those of the curse enough. I had learned to highly appreciate those moments.

"I'm sorry for whatever I did to make you uncomfortable. I know I can be a lot sometimes," I said with a shrug.

She had still been looking at the treats, but her head shot up when I said that. "You're sorry?" she asked with surprise.

"Of course I am. I made a bad impression on you and I'm trying to fix it, if you'll let me."

She shook her head slowly, and my heart sank until she said, "You have nothing to apologize for. Me, on the other hand … I strong armed you into helping me in the library and then assaulted you, and bit you. Gods, I actually bit you."

She was too damned adorable. The blush that crept up her neck was just icing on top of an already perfect cake. She didn't seem to see the humor in what she had said. Instead, she looked incredibly upset and serious, so I tried to hold back, but I shook with laughter. She looked up, startled.

"Princess, if that's what you consider assault, I would beg to be abused by you."

She smiled a little, saying, "I just got carried away."

"You can get carried away all over me whenever you'd like. Ravish me, princess."

She chuckled at that, and in a flash, grabbed a cinnamon roll and chucked it at my head. I didn't even see it until it was in the air. Luckily, I had quick reflexes. I caught it a moment before impact. I glanced at it, considering. I could take a bite, but where would be the fun in that? Looking her dead in the eyes, I stuck out my tongue at her before slowly licking some of the frosting from the roll.

I felt her watching me and heard her utter, "Gods forgive me," before launching herself at me. I just barely had time to drop the cinnamon roll to catch her before she was in my arms with her lips on mine.

She kissed me with reckless abandon, like I was the air she needed to breathe. I kissed her back just as hard, hoping she would never stop. I wrapped my arms around her, but she pulled away from the kiss.

Anxious she was going to run like last time, I quickly opened my eyes, but she was smiling at me. She took a strand of my hair and twisted it in her fingers. "I love how it changes colors in the light." She twirled it. "Right now, it looks royal blue, but if I look at it this way," she twisted it again, "it looks sapphire."

I watched her, waiting for her to pull out of my arms, but she didn't.

"What?" she asked when she noticed I was still staring.

"You're not running."

She laughed. "I don't actually do that often."

I smirked. "Only with me then?"

Her gaze moved from my hair to my eyes. "What can I say? You bring out a feisty side of me."

"I love it."

She cocked an eyebrow at me. "There you go again, trying to make me run. It's a little early for you loving me, don't you think?"

I paled, and she burst into laughter. "Don't worry. I'm not going anywhere for a while. I planned to stay awhile, and I'm not changing my plans for you," she said with a grin.

I didn't feel I knew her well enough to ask what her plans were, but I would take any of the time she gave me.

Chapter Nine

The next week flew by with her by my side. Her habits didn't change. She still slept most of the day away, but now she spent most of her nights with me. I started sleeping in and staying up later, adapting as best I could to her schedule to spend more time with her. I didn't know what I had done to be lucky enough to capture her attention, but I was grateful for it.

We spent a lot of time reading together, enjoying each other's company. I had been helping her pick out some books that I thought she might like, but she wasn't making it easy. She still wouldn't tell me what types of books she enjoyed, but I recommended a few of my favorites to her that she thankfully seemed to enjoy.

I sighed with relief when I finished the last of my tasks for the day, knowing that meant I could join her soon. The days were for work, but my evenings where reserved for Loralie. I took the book I was reading, closed the desk for the night, and went to the den to meet her. The nights were getting chillier, so I lit a fire and set up some blankets near the chairs by the fire in case she got cold. I settled in and started my book, waiting for her. She sauntered in with one of the books I had picked for her, forgoing the chair I had set out for her, and walked over to me.

"Aren't you going to make room for me?"

I looked in confusion at the other chair. "I put out a chair for you."

She looked at me pointedly before turning around. I thought she was going to the other chair, but she lowered herself into my lap. Not the most practical for reading, but far preferable.

I pulled her closer, making sure she was secure. "This is why you're in charge, princess."

She laughed at that, and my heart soared. "I do have good ideas, don't I?"

"The best."

Not even a moment later, Coal jumped up onto the other chair and set about making himself at home kneading his paws into the blanket laying on the chair. I chuckled softly to myself and pulled Loralie closer to me. I knew neither of us would have moved him anyway.

Cuddled up that close, between her kisses and her jasmine scent clouding my thoughts, I didn't get much reading done. I doubt she did either, but the night was perfect anyway.

I took her on a moonlight stroll one night through the gardens. We walked the lanes, talking and laughing. I was happy to be in her company. I pointed out some of the different flowers and plants to her, and was surprised when she didn't seem to be familiar with most of them.

Of course, Char had introduced me to some of the stranger plants and herbs that I hadn't known. After all, you didn't grow up in an apothecary without knowing a lot about plants, and he loved teaching others new things. I was sure if he ever found out Loralie needed an herbal education, he would talk her into the grave.

It turned out that I found joy in it, too. Showing her each new flower and plant and watching the delighted wonder on her face was nothing short of magical.

"I can't believe you have so many beautiful plants here. It's incredible! So beautiful!"

"You're so beautiful," I said, grinning.

She chuckled and rolled her eyes, "I wasn't fishing for compliments, but the beauty here is remarkable."

I looked around the garden again, trying to see it from her perspective, from fresh eyes. I knew it was pretty, but beautiful? Breathtaking? To me, it just looked like rows of neatly planted hedges, plants, and flowers, well maintained and pretty, but not remarkable.

"You must have had something like this where you grew up," I said. As it left my mouth, I realized my mistake and grimaced. Her shoulders had tightened. Lor didn't like talking about her past. I understood of course, I wasn't exactly open about all of mine either.

I looked around wildly for something else to say and was surprised when she spoke. "Flowers, plants in general, don't grow too well back home. Where I used to live," she hurriedly corrected herself. She was a lost soul like me. I knew what she meant. It was hard to really call anywhere home, to claim anywhere. It only made it hurt that much more when it was wrenched away from you.

Most days I tried not to think of home, but being around Lor made me feel sentimental.

"Back where I'm from, flowers, gardens like this aren't supposed to exist, but the pal-" I stopped short, catching myself before saying palace. I didn't want to share that part of my past with her. It would only put her in danger if anyone from Bancroft were to find us. Better to keep her in the dark. "...place where I'm from," I amended, "had gardens, not quite as beautiful as this, but magical in their own right by their sheer impossibility."

"Oh," she said, nodding, "So they were magic?"

I blinked a moment at that. They weren't magic, at least not in the way she meant. Altea's ruling families had never shared in the gifts of the other Realms. They didn't have any sort of power to speak of, so while Altea didn't used to shun magic, the Realm had learned to function without it through the use of machinery. When magic was abundant, magic had been used to aid the machines, but Altea had never been dependent on it. Which was a blessing now that the shield was up and magic no longer worked within the Realm.

The ruling families hadn't allowed a reliance on magic, saying it was too fickle and could be taken away. I was sure they were happy for their preparations now.

Altea was the only Realm that didn't rely on magic. My parents often talked of trying to spread our knowledge but the other Realms weren't interested, saying there was no need for a magic-less life.

I didn't like keeping things from Loralie, but if Bancroft found me, the less she knew, the better. I couldn't tell her about the machinery that ran the gardens, that would be as good as waving the Altean flag in her face. So, although the gardens weren't magic, I nodded.

She smiled at that, and I hoped she didn't notice my own smile had dimmed.

Thankfully, she was quick to distract me. She led me to the lilies and jasmine, saying they were her favorite. No surprise there.

"They remind me of you," I had told her.

She squealed at that, and launched herself at me, wrapping her hands behind my neck, pulling me down and kissing me hard.

As time wore on, I became more used to Lor's patterns and was starting to be able to anticipate her needs. She was still unpredictable, but I quickly learned two undeniable truths about her; she never woke earlier than midday and she was a grouch until she had coffee.

She called it her morning coffee, and it didn't help her grouchiness when I corrected her that it was midday coffee since the sun had been up for hours. She had the same habit of calling her first meal of the day breakfast despite it usually being around the end of the day.

When she came into the kitchen around late afternoon, looking tired, I couldn't help but laugh. She rubbed her eyes, and asked, "What are you making?"

"Dinner for those of us that keep normal schedules."

She laughed at that. "So breakfast? Wonderful!"

I gave her an exaggerated eye roll, but couldn't hide my smile for long.

She moved behind me, pressed herself against my back, and wrapped her arms around me. She placed a kiss on my cheek asking, "What can I do to help?"

I chuckled, and seeing she was still half asleep, waved off her offer.

She pouted. "I can help," she insisted.

After a moment, I told her, "There is something you can do."

She yawned again before saying, "Anything."

Before she could protest, I lifted her up and set her on the counter next to me.

"Hey!" she protested but she was smiling. I cut off the rest of her protests with a deep kiss. I regrettably had to pull away to focus on the meal.

She groaned when I pulled away, but there would be plenty of time for that later. I just smiled and grabbed her mug. Any pretense of her annoyance left her face when I handed her the cup of coffee I already had waiting for her.

She gave me a sleepy smile as she sat there and savored her coffee, content to sit back and watch me work. I was happy to cook for her. She deserved better than I could give her, but this was something I could easily do for her. I wanted to spoil her, in more ways than one.

Except, while we were getting closer, there was still a line both her and I seemed reluctant to cross. We shared the nights together, but she never invited me to her room, and I didn't dare invite her to mine. The last thing I wanted was to speed things up. I wanted to enjoy the beginning of this. The beginning of something so new, so fragile. We were so happy. I didn't want it to end. I didn't want the bubble to burst.

I was happier than I had been in a long time, and so far, I had somehow kept the curse at bay, but I could feel it hovering over my every interaction with her, waiting to strike. The more serious this got, the more dangerous it became. I didn't understand why the curse was allowing me the freedom to take things slowly with her.

Now I realize what I couldn't at the time; it was inevitable. The curse didn't push me further because her and I were already trapped. From the first moment I saw her, I knew she would be trouble, and I was right.

CHAPTER TEN

It took another couple of days before I couldn't hold back anymore, couldn't resist the compulsions of the curse any longer. Unfortunately for me, I couldn't have picked a worse day.

When she came wandering down the stairs that night, I was already waiting with her coffee and a cinnamon bun. Baking helped with my guilt. I had been doing a lot of baking since she showed up.

If I was going to have to share this with her, curse her with this, then at least I would treat her to something delicious first.

She smiled, taking first the coffee and then the treat, her eyes sparkling. "How did you know?"

"Know what?"

"What today is," she said quietly.

"What's today?"

She smiled. "Yeah, okay, like you just have treats and coffee waiting for me right when I wake up every day."

"I could if you wanted it."

She laughed at that. "I don't know how you knew, but I'm glad you do. I never really celebrate anymore. It's been a while since

I've had someone to share it with, but I'm happy to share it with you." She smiled and pulled me in for a kiss.

I racked my brain but couldn't come up with any explanation for what today was.

When she pulled back, she said, "Since you're too polite to ask the number, I'll tell you, I'm twenty-nine today."

Fuck. It was her damned birthday. Of all days, her birthday had to be today. I tried to get myself to move, to run away from her, to leave the room. She'd be hurt, but she might understand eventually. I couldn't do this to her today. Not on her birthday. Especially not when she'd just been saying how badly she wanted to have a happy day.

Unfortunately, I had used up all my strength and willpower fighting the curse; I didn't have enough fight in me to stop it. It was already in motion.

A predatory smile crept over my face. I hated myself right now, more than I ever had. More even than in the aftermath of Zara's death. I despised myself.

"There's something I want you to have and something I need you to know about me."

"Ooohh, a present? You shouldn't have!" she said with a delighted smile.

"I've been holding myself back from doing this. I didn't know how things were going to go between us, but I know now that I can't hold back from you anymore. I need you to have this." I tried to say something, anything that might warn her, but nothing came out. I tried to stop myself, but my hand reached of its own accord for the key in the pocket it was always in. As I touched the smooth, cold metal, I felt my heart race. *Let go,* I kept telling myself, but my hand wouldn't listen. Against my will, my hand drew the key out and pressed it in her hand.

"A key?" she asked. She took it in her hand, turning it over, inspecting it.

A moment later, she looked back up at me, confused. "I don't get it."

I just watched her, waiting.

She looked back at the key again, tracing the metal before saying, "Wait I know! Does the key unlock my present's hiding spot?"

"No!" I yelled, alarmed.

She looked startled by my outburst and laughed nervously. "Okay, okay, so the key is the gift." She looked at it perplexed for a moment before asking, "Is this what I think it is?"

I watched as her shoulders stiffened and her body tensed. A piece of her hair had fallen over her eyes. With a calm I didn't feel, I reached over and gently tucked it behind her ear. "What do you think it is, princess?"

"Are you asking me to move in with you?" I was so startled I didn't say a word. "I know we've been getting to know each other lately, but I'm not ready for that. We haven't even spent the night together."

"You mean the day?" I couldn't stop myself from teasing her. We both laughed and some of the tension eased from her body. "But no, that's not what that's for."

She looked relieved and perplexed, continuing to look at the key for any clues. "So, what is it for?"

"It opens room 13."

"What's in room 13?"

Now was my chance to scare her off, my chance to tell her, but try as hard as I might, I couldn't say a word. Instead, I felt my shoulders raise into a shrug and said, "A storage of sorts, for all my worst secrets."

"Ahh, it's where you hide the skeletons in the closet," she said, nodding.

Internally, I was screaming. How could she possibly know that? Why was she so nonchalant about it? Wouldn't that scare her off? A moment later, she started laughing. "So, what's really in room 13?"

"I hope you never find out. In giving this to you, I'm trusting you with my life and all my secrets. I need you to promise me you'll protect it and never use it, no matter what. If you truly care about me, you won't open the door."

She cocked her head with a smile, fingering the key in her hand. "So why give me the key at all? Is this a test?"

I shook my head quickly. "It's the most serious thing in the world to me."

"Okay, so I'm just supposed to hold on to this key for the rest of my time here, however long, without question? Without having any idea what it is I'm protecting?"

I nodded. "By protecting that, you're protecting me."

She watched me carefully for a minute, likely waiting for some sign I was joking, but she wouldn't find any. I was deadly serious. After a few moments, she rolled her eyes and laughed. "Okay, weirdo, I'll play whatever game this is."

My eyes followed as she slid the key provocatively over her cleavage before plunging it into her corset. When she looked up and saw I was still watching, her eyes brightened. "For safekeeping," she said with a wink.

A feeling of dread sank in that she might not understand the seriousness of this, but how could she? She didn't know what a monster I was. She had no idea, or she would never let me touch her. She pulled me close and kissed me deeply. I sank into her, savoring her, before she pulled away. "Next time, I do accept books or jewelry as gifts," she said, laughing.

"I'll take that under advisement," I said, smirking, unable to stay serious for too long around her. MaybeI was worrying too much. Maybe she would be the one to save me.

Chapter Eleven

I had been putting off Char meeting Loralie for as long as I could, but I knew it was killing him and that he wouldn't be denied much longer.

The only reason I had gotten away with it so far was that he was very much a morning person and she woke with the sunset, but I knew my luck wasn't going to continue, so I finally decided that arranging the meeting on my own terms was a better alternative to whatever scheme Char would come up with.

I invited him to dinner, and it was hard to tell whether him or Lor were more excited.

He came over early with some herbs his mom was able to spare. She was always sending him along with a little something for me. As kind as it was, it made me miss my own family that much more.

I was almost done with dinner, and per usual Lor hadn't come down yet, but I wasn't worried. I knew how excited she was to meet Char. I would go wake her pretty soon if she didn't come down, but I hoped I wouldn't have to. She was a grouch when she didn't get to sleep as long as she liked.

He followed me into the kitchen and leaned against the counter, watching me work.

"So, things are going good?" he asked, trying to seem casual, but there was no hiding the excitement in his voice.

I wasn't sure how to answer that. Objectively, things were going really well. I was incredibly happy with her and I had no reason to think that she didn't trust me, to think she might be in danger. But I would be lying if I didn't say that her having the key wasn't weighing heavily on my mind.

"What's wrong?" he asked quickly, taking a step closer and examining my face. I was never good at hiding the emotions on my face, at least not when the curse wasn't in control.

"It's hard to explain. I really care about her and love spending time with her."

"But...?"

"But I'm feeling how I did about Zara about Lor, maybe worse." It was the best way I could think to describe it, but that was exactly the problem. I had fallen hard for her and now that the curse had her, I was scared for her.

"I know what you mean, but I think you're wrong. Just because someone hurt you in the past, doesn't mean you're not worthy of being loved. Lor seems like a smart girl. She has to be if she sees how special you are."

My smile started to come back. I couldn't stay upset for long with Char around. "Thanks man, I really like her."

I was searching for how else to describe my feelings when I saw Char's eyes light up and his grin magnify.

I turned around and saw Lor making her way over to us. She was wearing her favorite casual gown, a crimson red corset and overskirt paired over a flowy white underdress. It seemed silly to me that she called it casual, but compared to her other dresses it certainly covered more of her.

She moved toward us and seemed to pause for a moment wondering how to greet Char, but he closed the distance and wrapped her in a hug, picking her up and twirling her in a circle. Her giggles were music to my ears.

The entire dinner, they were thick as thieves and I loved it. It warmed my heart that the both of them were getting along so well. Outside of Altea, Char was the only family I had. It meant the world to me that he liked Lor.

As we sat there eating, and I listened to them laughing and telling stories and jokes, I realized I had lied to Char. What I felt for Lor wasn't anything like what I felt for Zara. I had been infatuated with Zara. Lor was different. I was in love with Lor.

I pulled out the wine and packed it along with some sweets in a basket. I made my way from the kitchen toward the stairs, stopping in the den to grab a blanket and slinging it over my arm.

The sun was just starting to set, so I scrawled a quick note for Lor and slipped it under her door before making my way to the garden.

I went to a few spots, but none of them felt right. By the time the sun had fully set and the stars were starting to come out, I had found the perfect spot. I quickly made my way to the ring of trees and ducked under the branches of a large purple flowered tree into the hidden clearing within. The trees were in a tight circle growing toward each other, their branches stretching up toward the sky entangled in each other. There was a gap in their cover that let you gaze up at the stars. It was perfect.

I quickly laid out the blanket and the basket, and made my way back to the main garden path. Lor should be here any minute, but there was no way she would find the place on her own, especially since my note had only told her to dress for an outdoor surprise and head to the garden.

When I found her, she was just entering the garden. She was wearing a dark blue silk dress with stars embroidered on it that stole my breath for a moment. I pulled her in for a kiss. We stayed there a while before she pulled away.

"So, what's this surprise you have for me?" she asked, aglow with excitement.

"You'll have to come with me and find out." I took her hand and led her through garden paths one turn after another until we arrived at the circle of trees.

She gasped and reached out to gently stroke one of the purple blooms on the tree. "It's beautiful," she whispered reverently.

I brushed a strand piece of hair behind her ear and planted a kiss on her forehead. "Follow me."

I squeezed her hand and pulled her under the branches with me. When she saw the blanket and basket, her eyes widened. I let go of her hand and crossed the small clearing to the basket. I reached in and pulled out two glasses and the wine, pouring wine into both of them before turning back and offering one to her.

In the glint of the moonlight, I saw a couple of tears run down her cheeks, but she was smiling wide. She closed the distance and took the glass I held out for her.

We drank the whole bottle while gorging on sweets and stargazing.

She cuddled close and I could feel her heartbeat quicken as she whispered, "I love you."

She loved me. This adorable perfection of a woman loved me. I didn't know how I was so lucky. I was grinning like a fool.

Before I could say anything, she started giggling. "That was an inside thought, but it ended up on the outside."

I laughed at that. "You're pretty drunk, aren't you?"

She pouted. "I'm not, you're drunk!"

I couldn't stop laughing and a moment later she laughed, too.

I pulled her closer to me, not wanting her any further than she already was. I kissed her cheek, and then softly asked, "You want to know a secret?"

"Oh! I love secrets!" she squealed.

"I love you, too, and I'm a little drunk, too."

One minute I was holding her and the next she was on top of me, kissing me.

Eventually, she fell asleep on my chest. I didn't want to risk waking her, so I stayed out until the stars started to dim with early morning light. Then I scooped her up and carried her through the garden and into the Inn. She didn't wake until I was on the stairs. I told her to go back to sleep, I was happy to carry her all the way to her room, but she wouldn't hear of it and started to slip out of my arms. I set her down on the ground and she gave me a sleepy goodnight kiss before heading to her room.

Chapter Twelve

Each new night that passed without incident was a small miracle. I thanked the gods every time I saw her safe and happy.

Maybe for once things would go my way. Maybe she would listen and things would be okay.

We had fallen into a blissful routine. Around nightfall, she would come wandering downstairs to see me. I greeted her with coffee and whatever I had been baking that day. It didn't matter to her that it was her first meal of the day or that it was essentially all sugar; she scarfed down whatever I made her.

She loved chocolate and was happy to have anything chocolate, but that was nothing compared to the way her face lit up when I made her my cinnamon rolls. Eventually, she told me it wasn't just because they were amazing, they were, but that wasn't why she was so excited for them. She loved them so much because she had decided they were our dessert. I hadn't known couples to pick and claim a dessert, but as long as she smiled like that, I would go along with whatever she wanted.

We passed most of our time together taking walks through the garden in the moonlight and reading by the fire in the den. With quite a few passionate kisses in between. Days passed into weeks with no mention of the room and no mention of her leaving. I stopped feeling as worried, stopped waiting for the worst to happen. I should have known better. When she didn't come down at her normal time, I thought nothing of it at first. It wasn't until I noticed her coffee was getting cold that I started to get worried. Even still, I thought I'd give her a few more minutes before going to check on her.

That was when I felt it, and all the blood drained from my body. That little tingling in the back of my neck and the urge to go to room 13. This couldn't be happening... I had gotten too comfortable. Let my guard down too much, let her get too comfortable, and now I was going to pay for it. We both were. Her more so than me.

I couldn't do this. I wouldn't. I tried grabbing the desk with my hands to hold my body there, but my feet were already moving. I was internally kicking and screaming, trying whatever I could to stop myself. I couldn't reach the room. She would find some way to escape, and we could pretend this never happened. Things could go back to normal. Everything would be okay as long as I didn't open that door. But my feet wouldn't stop.

I was surprised when I felt tears coming down my face. Normally, the curse took complete control, stifling my emotions. But I was fighting with everything I had to stop my feet from moving. The curse must not have had the extra energy to force me not to cry. I let that give me a little spark of hope and redoubled my efforts to stop, but if anything, my pace seemed to speed up.

I was up the stairs and halfway down the hallway when a door opened right in front of me. Her door. I saw her raven hair and stopped dead in my tracks. She was smiling until she looked up at me and her face fell. She reached up for my face and wiped a tear away with her thumb.

"What's wrong, love?"

"Nothing at all. You're here, you're safe, you're fine. Thank the gods. I'm alright now." I felt the pull of the curse again and knew I didn't have much longer. I pulled her close, hugging her tight, and kissed the top of her head before releasing her and pulling back. "I'm alright. I promise. I just have to go take care of something real quick."

I started to walk away, but she grabbed my hand. "Wait. What was wrong? Where are you going?"

"Everything will be fine. I just have to take care of something. In Room 13."

"13? But you said not to go in there."

I couldn't stop my legs from moving toward the room, but I was able to turn my head to see her. "I did, and you shouldn't, ever."

"But how are you even going to get in? I have the key!"

"The door will open for me. I'll come find you once I'm done, once it's safe."

I could see the battle on her face about whether to follow me.

With one last burst of will, I added, "Trust me, please. Don't follow me."

She looked torn, but after a moment's hesitation, nodded.

Relieved, I stopped fighting and let my feet carry me the rest of the way there. I wondered what nightmare I was walking into, but I didn't really care anymore. Whoever it was, it wasn't her.

I grasped the doorknob and felt the handle's zap before it sprung open. I turned and closed it behind me as quickly as I could. Only after I had relocked the door and put the deadbolt in place did I turn around.

On the bed, sprawled out and waiting, was our maintenance man. Fuck. How many times had I told the cleaning crew in explicit detail to leave this room alone? I had told everyone that anyone who so much as looked at the door for too long would be fired. Most had been happy to not have the extra room to clean, others thought the request was weird, but they all stayed clear of the room, or they all had, until now.

I gaped at him on the bed. This wasn't how things were supposed to happen. I was supposed to fall for them, make them fall for me, give them the key, and then murder them if they used it. He wasn't invited in; he shouldn't be here.

His eyes looked like they were about to pop out of their sockets and tears ran down his face. I heard muffled noises from him and realized he was gagged. That wasn't all. He was bound to the four-poster bed.

Either someone had done some of the work for me already, or the curse didn't like his being here anymore than I did. I watched as his arm almost broke loose only for the sheets to tighten around him Apparently the curse didn't take kindly to intruders.

It was waiting for Loralie and wasn't happy that someone else had interrupted.

I'd only done this once since the curse started, but I had thought I knew what to expect.

This was certainly new, and I had no idea how he had gotten in. There was only one key to the room, that Loralie still had. There wasn't any reason for him being in here. Everyone on my staff knew this room was expressly forbidden. I had heard all sorts of rumors about what I might be keeping in here or doing in here, but everyone knew it was off limits.

The pull of the curse had subsided a little now that I was in the room, thankfully. I took a minute to look around and noticed that next to the door at my feet there were a few metal tools and a sack. I leaned down to get a better look and after a moment, I pieced it together, but I wanted confirmation. The curse wouldn't let me leave, wouldn't let me spare him, but I hoped he might at least assuage my guilt a little.

I knew him well enough to know he was a loner. He always worked the odd shifts since he had no one waiting for him at home. At least I wasn't taking someone's husband or father away from them. I wouldn't enjoy this, but I was grateful the situation wasn't worse.

Honestly, it could have been anyone. As long as it wasn't her, I would have been grateful. I peeled the gag out of his mouth, and he started to scream in earnest. I knew it would do him no good. No noise ever seemed to escape the room. The curse made sure of it.

"I'm so sorry, but I'm going to need you to quiet down. I would like some answers from you, but I don't need them. If you continue screaming, I will put this back in."

He looked at me in horror and quieted down, but didn't stop talking. "Ma'am, thank the gods you're here! I don't know who cast a spell on this room, but the moment I entered and saw the bodies, I started screaming my head off, but the sheets sprung to life and grabbed me. I kept screaming, but then I was gagged. I'm so glad you heard me. Please help me."

"What were you doing in here, anyway? This room is dangerous."

"I can see that now, ma'am. I'm so sorry. I never would have come in if I had known."

"But you did know. I've told everyone on my staff numerous times that this room is off limits. What compelled you to enter?"

"I had forgotten. I thought this was room 12 and was just coming in to fix the window latch. Please help me." His voice was rising as he tried to get his hands loose.

"But the room was locked. How did you get in?"

"The door was open. You have to believe me."

I rolled my eyes and walked back over to the door, picking up the tools and the sack. If I hadn't seen the evidence myself, I might have believed his lies.

The curse took control. I couldn't stop it. I looked over at Alanna and Zara's bodies, and let out a humorless laugh. "What do we think, ladies? Do we believe him?"

He looked at me, terrified, speechless. I was disgusted with myself. I tried not to look at the bodies when I could help it. The curse kept them horrifically, perfectly preserved, and it was unnerving and always served to bring about feelings of guilt and grief.

More so with Zara than Alanna, but even with Alanna there was some guilt, and still some anger for her betrayal. It wasn't her fault, per se, but in a way she had ruined my life. Yes, I had taken her life, but the consequences were still haunting me, so most days I considered us even.

I sauntered over to him and dropped the tools and sack on his chest. "This doesn't look very much like cleaning equipment."

"Please, please. I'm so sorry. I only needed some money. I was hoping to sell whatever you kept so guarded, but I promise I never would have intruded if I had known, and I won't tell a soul about anything I saw. Please, please, please," he begged, on the verge of hysteria.

"So, the salary I pay you is worthless enough that you needed to resort to stealing from me. Whatever happened to asking for a raise?"

"I never meant to disrespect you, ma'am. Please help me and I swear I won't breathe a word of this to anyone."

I shrugged. "Well, if I don't help you, you won't have the chance to breathe a word of it to anyone."

I was toying with him and hated it. I knew he wasn't going to be able to leave the room. The curse wouldn't let me let him. I hoped I could at least make it quick, but something felt different about this time. It wasn't like with Zara; there hadn't been much time allowed for talking or for goodbyes. I would have killed for the chance to have said goodbye, the chance to explain myself. At least I hadn't drawn it out with her, but I didn't know why the curse was letting me take things slowly this time. Why was he still breathing?

It wasn't until my hand started inching toward a lock pick that the realization and horror set in. This wasn't how things were supposed to go. I was supposed to strangle him like I did with Alanna, starting the whole curse in motion, but nothing about this was normal. He wasn't even supposed to be here. I grimaced, hoping I at least wouldn't make too much of a mess.

All the while, he was still wasting his breath pleading for forgiveness and freedom, both of which wouldn't come. "Please, please, let me go. You don't have to do this! Please! Help me!"

I couldn't decide if his speech was for me anymore or if he hoped for some rescue, but none would come. I picked up the tool, holding it in my hand, spinning it around until it caught his eye.

His screams increased in volume as I ran the metal over his face, circling around one eye and then the other. I hoped the curse wouldn't really make me stab his eyes out. I felt a bit of relief when my hand took the tool further south and stopped over his heart.

I pulled it back and looked at him. "Be a good boy and hold still. You won't feel a thing." I winked at him. He started flailing and fighting in earnest then, but the magic held up and the sheets kept him pinned down. I shrugged. "Well, there you go, moving all about. This is really going to hurt now. Don't say I didn't warn you."

A moment later, I moved the tool back and plunged it into his heart. The blood spurted out quickly. I felt him twitching under me for a few moments and twisted the metal into him harder. After another moment, he stopped moving altogether and deadly silence returned to the room.

I wanted to collapse in a heap on the floor. I felt like hyperventilating. I had taken two lives before, but never so violently. I would have been uselessly curled up in a corner if it wasn't for the curse. I was thankful for that; I didn't have time to spare. I was sure Loralie would come looking for me if I was gone much longer.

I also couldn't have any evidence leave the room, but the curse had already taken care of that. I knew I had had blood on me, could still feel its presence on me, but when I looked down, all the traces of blood on me were gone. A quick glance at the bed showed that the sheets and bed didn't get the same treatment. I had never stabbed someone before, so I couldn't be sure what might happen when I left the room. I wondered if the room would still look the same if I had to come back in.

A moment later, I realized the implication and shuddered at the thought. I wouldn't have to come back in. Loralie wouldn't open the door. She couldn't. But how could I ever really be sure of that? Visions of the past few minutes played out in my mind with her there instead, and I wanted to scream.

I had gotten so lucky this time that it wasn't her, but how long would I stay lucky? I had never thought Zara would open the door, and look where she was now, sitting with Alanna.

But Loralie was different, right? She had to be. I had never felt this strongly about anyone before. She had to be the one, right?

But was I willing to risk her life over being wrong?

Even if I wanted to, was there any way I could get her to leave? I couldn't say for sure. But I cared too much about her to keep her in any danger if there was a choice.

If there was a choice, I would choose to be alone and miserable instead of having her wind up dead. If I could get her to leave, I knew I should. No matter how wrong it felt, it was the right thing to do. I felt the tears running down my face and knew I would have to try, and soon, before I lost my nerve.

I couldn't tell her any more of the curse, but maybe I could caution her away.

Chapter Thirteen

I had to go find her. I stood and made my way to the door, feeling unsteady on my feet. A wave of nausea came over me at the sight of all the blood. His death would haunt me just like the others' deaths had. Not because his death was particularly meaningful to me, like theirs had been, but because of how gruesome it was. I wouldn't soon forget how warm and sticky his blood felt coating my skin.

I stumbled out of the room, taking care to shut the door tightly behind me. The last thing I wanted was someone stumbling on the open door.

I headed for my room, wanting to change. I knew there wasn't any blood on me anymore, but I still felt like there was. A nice change of clothes might go a long way to making me feel more refreshed.

But when I opened the door, Loralie was waiting there for me.

She ran into my arms, but not before I noticed the tears streaming down her face. I hugged her for a long moment before pulling away.

"What's wrong, Lor? What happened?"

She stared at me in disbelief. "What do you mean, what happened? You terrified me!"

A relieved sigh came out before I told her, "I'm okay. I promise I'm fine." It wasn't a lie, I was more or less fine now that I knew she was safe.

She glared at me. "You can't just show up out of the blue terrified and crying and expect me not to worry." Her gaze softened and she stroked my chin with her thumb as she examined my face. "What happened, love? Are you okay?"

I nodded quickly. "I am. I swear I am."

"So, what happened?!"

I hesitated for a moment, trying to get the words out, but they wouldn't come. "I can't really explain."

"First you terrify me, and now you won't even give me an explanation. I just have to trust that you're fine and everything's fine now?"

"It's not that I don't want to tell you," I said carefully. I was at war with myself. I could try to warn her again, but then she would leave. But I still felt the blood on my skin, still felt sticky and like the stench of death clung to me. After all this time, I could still feel my fingers wrapping around Zara's throat as she pleaded with me for her life and I couldn't do a damn thing to stop myself. I couldn't do this.

I couldn't do this to Lor. She deserved so much better than me and I would be even more of a monster than I already was if I let her stay. "It's that I can't tell you, but what I can tell you is-" I tried a few versions of the words and eventually was able to push enough past the curse to say, "I'm a monster."

She looked surprised for a moment, some of the anger dimming from her eyes, before she took my hand. "That's not true. I don't know what made you believe that, but there's only one monster in this room and it most definitely isn't you," she said with a sad smile.

I shook my head. "Loralie, listen to me. You could never be a monster. You don't know the first thing about evil. I..." Tears started streaming down my face as I tried to push out any words that might make her understand. "It's..." I was struggling hard. Fighting against the curse and my will.

I didn't want her to leave, but she needed to. Her life was more important than my happiness, and I had been a gods damned fool to let things get this far. It could've been her in the room today. Thank the gods it wasn't, but it was too close. I couldn't let her stay. "You're not safe here," I was finally able to get out.

"Not safe? What are you talking about? Are you asking me to leave?"

I bit my tongue hard; the curse was fighting back, pushing me to take it back. Tears still streaming down my face, I nodded.

"That's it? You just want me to pack my things and move on? Without a single explanation, you just don't want me anymore?" She sighed, and a tear slipped down her face. "I shouldn't really be surprised. This always happens sooner or later once someone gets to know me. They always tire of me."

My heart broke into a million pieces. I was the worst type of trash in the Six Realms, Bancroft included. I let her get too close and now I was hurting her. I couldn't even stop myself in time before I said, "Lor, it's not like that. I will regret this every day for the rest of my life, but you can't stay."

She looked up at me, her face damp from her tears, confused. "Why?"

"I can't tell you."

She exploded. "You have to be fucking kidding me! You're just going to let us go and you can't even give me an explanation? You owe me an explanation!"

I did. I wished I could, but I just shook my head.

She glared at me a moment before something changed in her eyes. Looking determined and terrifying, she stalked past me to the door.

"I won't let you do this."

I watched the door close, debating whether I should go after her. I couldn't possibly make things worse, but maybe I should give her some space. I sighed and dragged my feet back to the bed, conflicted. I had hurt her, much more than I meant to, much more than I thought I would. I knew getting her to leave would destroy me, but I hadn't thought it would bother her as much.

A moment later, it occurred to me to be worried about what she might do, but when I felt the tingling on the back of my neck, I realized with horror that I was already too late.

I should have known. I should have known what she was going to do and should have stopped her. How could I have been so stupid? Of course when I wouldn't tell her anything, she would have thought about the key, of Room 13 that I told her contained all my secrets.

I gripped the bed hard, trying to keep myself stationary, but I felt the itch start in my feet and felt them move of their own accord, felt my hands let go of the bed and my body betray me, getting up and crossing the room involuntarily.

It took far quicker than I would have liked to get to room 13. I was internally screaming at my body to stop, to slow, anything, but I wasn't in control. When I touched the doorknob for the second time today, it was still warm. I turned the door and burst inside, quickly closing it behind me.

I saw her sprawled out on the floor over the man I had just killed. She was making a weird noise in her shock. I cleared my throat. She whipped her head around, looking horrified, and then a moment later, relieved when she realized it was me. Her relief was like a dagger to my heart.

She was covered in blood. There was even blood on her face. She had more blood on her than the body did. I didn't have to look to see if any of it was hers. The curse would have sensed if she were weak. I knew she wasn't injured.

I wanted to ask her why she was covered in blood, but before I could say anything, she started blabbering hysterically. "Thank the gods you're here, love. I don't know what happened. One minute I opened the door and was turning to lock it behind me when I tripped and landed on whoever this was." She gestured to the body. "I tried resuscitating him before I saw where the blood was coming from. I have no idea what happened. He was like this when I came in. You have to believe me!"

"I do, princess. I know you didn't do this."

"Thank the gods you believe me. I know how this looks but-"

The curse took over. I couldn't fight it. A predatory smile spread over my face as I interrupted her. "You don't understand, princess. I know you didn't do this because I know who did."

"You do?" she asked, surprised. "Why haven't you called for help? We have to do something!"

I was trying to scream at her to leave, jump out the window, try to get out the door, anything, but I knew it was useless. Even if I could've gotten the words to come out, I was in front of the door, and it wouldn't be a pleasant fall from the second floor. She would at least break an ankle, only an ankle if she was lucky, and I would catch her before she could hobble away. There was no escape for her.

"You don't understand. There's nothing to be done."

She looked confused, before she took in the look on my face, and her own face paled more than usual. "You don't mean...?"

"Yes, princess. How do you like my handiwork?"

She stood up with a start and took a step back. "You can't mean that."

I took a step closer.

"Now you know my secret," I said with a grin. "There are no more secrets between us now. Actually, there is still one, what I'm going to do next, but I think that's pretty obvious."

My eyes fell to Alanna and Zara's bodies, when I looked back, I saw she had seen them too. Her already pale face paled further.

"What do you say girls? She would make a nice addition to my little collection, huh?"

She stilled. I advanced another step. *What is she doing? Run! Get away from me! Fight! Do something!* Another step. Only a few more and I would be within arm's reach of her.

She took a couple of quick steps back, hitting the bed and tumbling onto it. I sprung on her, straddling her body, and quickly pulled both her arms above her head. She didn't move, just stared at me in shock. *Fight me!* Didn't she realize what was happening? *Do something!* She couldn't overpower me, not usually, and certainly not with the curse controlling me, but why wasn't she fighting? Did she think I wanted to hurt her? That this was really me? I hoped she knew I would never willingly do this.

I leaned down and planted a couple of kisses on her neck. She shivered and leaned into my touch out of habit. "What a good little girl you are," I said with a purr. "Still so responsive. Even when you know it's not good for you, you still crave me. I wonder, will you even bother to fight me, or are you resigned to your fate?"

Fight me! I was screaming at her! *Fight me! Please, try anything!* I gestured with my free hand to Alanna and Zara's bodies. "They both fought me, little good it did them, but I'd love to see you try."

Try, gods damn it! Kill me if you have to! Stop me!

She looked up as a tear came down her face. "Why are you doing this?"

"Because, my dear princess, I'm a very bad girl." I tried as hard as I could to force out the truth, and was surprised when it came out. "The first time I took a life was Alanna over there. She was staying in this very room and was supposed to meet me for a romantic dinner, but she never showed.

When I came upstairs to check on her, I heard her moaning from down the hall. I was terrified for her and broke down the door in two kicks, only to find her riding some man I had never met. I saw red. I grabbed her, threw her off him, and didn't think twice about strangling the life out of her. It didn't occur to me to remember the man she was with until after she stopped breathing, but he was already gone.

Some man he was, leaving her to my mercy, not that I had any. He didn't even try to stop me. He must have really given a damn about her. She ruined everything between us and ended up dead all for a man who abandoned her to her fate. I hated her for that and couldn't bring myself to regret what I'd done.

A day later, I was trying to figure out what to do with the body, when a face appeared in the mirror. It was the most beautiful man I'd ever seen. His dark eyes swam with knowledge and a tinge of sadness. His dark hair was tousled and unkempt, but that didn't diminish his beauty. I couldn't stop staring at him, and when I was able to tear my eyes away from his, it was just to stare at his necklace. He was wearing an ornate ruby that glinted red and seemed to pulse with light. I watched it for a few moments before his eyes caught mine again.

He looked at me judgmentally and asked if I was Delphine. I nodded. He looked at the body and asked if I regretted it, and told me he would know if I was lying. I thought about lying. It seemed like the right thing to do. Who kills someone in cold blood and doesn't even regret it?"

I smiled down at her. "Me. I was truthful and shook my head. She had deserved it, I told him. I wouldn't regret taking her life when she had deserved it. A smile so sad came over his face that I wanted to cry. 'Very well,' he had said. 'I take no pleasure in this, but know you brought it upon yourself. When the huntsman showed up and told us of you, he tried to strike a deal, but I told him I would only hold up my end if you showed no remorse. I had hoped you might, but you clearly lack any. You will remember today as the start of the rest of your life, and if you ever think of me with anger, think of yourself with more. This could have been avoided with any regret.

From today forward, this room will be preserved for your eyes only. It will be your dirty little secret, a window into your soul and how much of a monster you are. You will want to keep this room a secret, but that's the curse. The moment you fall for another who cares about you in return, the moment you care about them more than yourself, you will have to give them the key to this room, the key to your soul and your dirty little secret.

You will warn them to stay out, but you cannot prevent them from entering. Whether they trust your warning and listen will be up to them, but if they do enter the room, they will not be able to leave alive. You will be compelled to follow them and to mercilessly end their lives the way you did to her.

The longer you go without caring about others, the lonelier you will become. You will be drawn to others and try to get them to be drawn to you as well. You will try to seduce them, keep them close, all so that one day, when you can't resist anymore, you will give them the key. There is no escape from the curse, not for you, not now, not ever. Although,' he had said with a sad smile, 'I know that doesn't mean you won't try. Here's a little reminder to make sure you can't go a day without remembering how much of a monster you are.' As he faded from the mirror, I watched in horror as my hair turned a vibrant shade of blue. It's been like that ever since," I said, using a strand of it to caress her neck. "So now you know my secret."

She didn't look nearly as horrified as I expected; she looked sad, for me or herself I couldn't tell. "Well, get it over with then, and know that, love, if you can hear me in there, I forgive you."

I was screaming at myself to stop. The curse wasn't strong enough to stop the tears from coming down my face. As I laced my hand around her neck, she didn't try to stop me. I forced out the words, coming out as a whisper, "I love you," as I tightened my hands around her neck. She looked at me with nothing but love until she stopped moving altogether, her eyes closing.

I started sobbing in earnest then as I slipped my hands from her neck, I kissed her forehead, still sobbing. "I'm so, so, so, so sorry. I won't ever forget you, Lor. I love you," I whispered, tears streaming down my face.

Half a heartbeat later, her eyes sprung open, and she smiled, "I love you, too," she replied with a wink.

I screamed, and before I could stop myself, my hand grabbed one of the leftover lock picks and plunged it into her heart. I screamed through my sobs. I had almost spared her, but I couldn't stop the curse. I moved away from her body, watching, waiting, hoping, but I knew she wouldn't move again. I could have sworn I had felt her stop breathing the first time, but I had run her through the heart this time. She wouldn't be moving again.

I tried to get my breathing under control; I needed to clean up the mess before I caused anyone alarm, but when I looked down, there wasn't any blood. The curse must have removed it already, but I didn't remember any in the first place. This was much more traumatic than killing the maintenance man earlier, but it felt different. I didn't remember any blood. There should have been blood.

I looked over at the bed and was shocked to find it empty. Had the curse moved her? It had never done that before. I looked over to where the other girls' bodies were, but she wasn't there. I was on the verge of hyperventilating. Had the curse really stolen what was left of her? I ran over to the bed, looking under it, thinking maybe she had fallen, but there was nothing there.

Then I felt a tap on my shoulder. I whirled around and saw her smiling at me. She took a step back, watching me cautiously. "Are we done with the stabbing?" she asked playfully.

"What? But you were...? Lor, is that really you?"

She smiled. "The one and only."

"But what...? You were just... you can't be. I have to be dreaming."

She smiled at me. "I'm better than a dream," she grinned, "but if you're quite done with the stabbing..." She looked warily behind me to the side table that held the rest of the lock picks. I waited to feel compelled to grab one, but nothing happened. I looked back at her in shock. She smiled. "Well then, since you showed me your secret, it's time you know mine." She started to leave the room, but I couldn't move. She noticed I wasn't following her and doubled back, taking my hand. "Come on, love. There's something I need to show you now."

I couldn't think, couldn't breathe, didn't dare say a word, waiting for this cruel dream to end. She led me out the door toward her room, passing through the threshold without any trouble. The curse had let her go. I didn't have time to ponder what that could mean for her, or for me, though since she continued to yank me down the hall to her room.

I had never been in her room before. Well, not since it had been occupied by her. She looked at me carefully and said, "This might be a bit of a shock to you, but I don't want there to be secrets between us, especially not now, and you've probably worked it out, anyway. You showed me yours, so I'll show you mine," she said with a wink and a giggle.

She took out her key and turned the lock. She looked over her shoulder, making sure the hallway was clear before opening the door and pushing me inside. She closed and locked the door quickly as I took in the room. The bed and furniture remained the same, but on every spare inch of the wall hung bags of a dark red liquid. I took a deep breath in, and the smell confirmed my suspicion. It was blood. I turned to look at her, only to see she had disappeared, but when I turned around again, she was in front of me, watching me carefully.

"So, now you understand?"

I gulped and nodded. This wasn't a dream. She hadn't died because she couldn't die. She was a vampire, and I was going to be her next meal. I deserved a fate like this. "Make it quick if you can," I said to her.

She frowned. "Just what do you think I'm going to do?"

"Well, I just tried to kill you, so I would assume you're going to drain every last drop from me. Just do it. I deserve it."

She looked at me carefully, weighing my words. "You did just try to kill me." She ran her tongue over her lips, parting them a little. I watched as her tongue traced over an extra sharp tooth. How had I not noticed her two sharp teeth before? I wondered, not able to tear my eyes from her tongue. "I really should make you pay." She stalked forward, power in her step, and I shrunk back. She pressed forward, her arms on my shoulders, and pushed me back. I hit the bed with an "ooof" before she was on top of me.

She smiled hungrily at me. "I could get used to this." She said, grazing my neck with her teeth, and licked a line up to my ear, whispering in it, "Love, this changes nothing. I'm not going to hurt you. I love you."

My jaw dropped. I searched her face for any sign this was a cruel joke, but she looked deadly serious, and happy. I started to cry, and she instantly moved from on top of me to lay beside me and pulled me close. "I'm so, so, so sorry. I thought I lost you. I thought I killed you. I'm so sorry; that wasn't me. I never wanted to hurt you. I love you."

"I love you, too," she said, stroking my hair as I cried. I felt a few of her tears dampen my face along with my own.. She smiled through her tears and said, "Lucky for you, I'm more durable than that."

"Incredibly durable." Looking around at the blood, I couldn't help but ask, "How many people did you have to drain for all this?"

She looked at me in shock for a moment. "You should know me better than that! I would never hurt someone if I didn't have to. You remember those men I brought up here?"

"Like I could forget how jealous it made me. I wanted to tear out their throats for having the audacity to hold your hand."

"So violent," she said with a laugh.

I shrugged sheepishly. "You bring that out in me."

"Good. I can handle it." She grinned before continuing, "Well, obviously, none of them died. I only take as much as they won't miss. It usually takes most of the night to drain them as much as I can and let them sleep it off. I've only gone too far once and won't ever do that again. Controlling myself can be harder sometimes than others. You make it hard for me to hold back sometimes."

A laugh went through me as I remembered the kiss in the library, when she bit me. "The kiss?"

She nodded. "The kiss. I ran because I was worried I would lose control, that I might hurt you, but I know better now. After the feeling I had today when you tried to end things, I know I would kill for you and I would die before seeing you hurt."

The meaning of her words caught up to me, and I screeched out, "You didn't know?" I said with a screech. "You didn't know if you'd survive and you let me try to kill you?"

She shrugged. "I thought I might be fine, but I can't say any-one's ever actually tried to kill me before. At least not in the few years I've been turned. But if I tried to stop you, I might have hurt you, and I would've rather been dead than have hurt you."

I started sobbing again.

"Promise me," I started through my tears. "Promise me from now on no secrets. From now on, if you'll have me, I'm yours, wholly and completely."

She grinned, tears still flowing as she leaned in and kissed me. She broke away far too quickly and said, "I promise. You are my heart and soul. Everything that I am is yours, wholly and completely."

I pulled her into my arms and held her close. From that day forward, I was never going to let her go. I don't know how I had known from the start, but I had. I had somehow known she was going to be different, and she was. She was my salvation, and I would worship her for the rest of our days.

Epilogue

A Few Months Later

When Lor came rushing into the kitchen in a panic, my blood froze. I quickly glanced behind her looking for danger, a chill racing up my spine. My wife, the unkillable vampire, didn't scare easily.

She rushed into my arms. I squeezed her a moment, before pulling away and looking at her.

"What's wrong?"

"I don't know how they found me, but I don't know if I can trust them. I have to hide. They can't find me. I don't know what they would do."

"Lor, slow down. Who's here? Who found you?"

"My nephew."

"Your nephew?!" I exclaimed loudly. She didn't have a nephew. She couldn't have a nephew. She had never even mentioned her family aside from her missing brother. "Your brother had a child?"

She shook her head, looking over her shoulder. "No. No. Not my brother, his husband."

This was the first I was hearing of her brother having a husband.

"I guess he's technically not my nephew." She rushed out, fiddling with her hands. "He's my brother's husband's nephew."

Well, that was a whole lot for what had started as a normal day.

"How do you know it's him?"

"A few Somerset soldiers just breezed in telling us to prepare our poor excuse for an inn for the honor of housing the Prince for a night. Can you believe the nerve? Prince or not, he's lucky to be staying at our inn, especially if you make him some of your kingdom famous cinnamon rolls."

My mind was racing a mile a minute trying to keep up. Her brother's husband's nephew was the Prince of Somerset. But that wasn't possible.

"But that's not possible. The King only has one brother..."

It hit me then all at once. The King of Somerset's brother was the King Killer himself, King Damien of Bancroft. The very same Damien that was the reason my Realm was in ruins and I was in hiding, separated from my family. He was the reason I was stuck here. He might not have cursed himself, but it was his fault I ended up here, his fault this happened to me. Even if the war ended and everything was safe, I couldn't leave and it was all his fault.

The fact that my wife was closely acquainted with the most notorious villain in the Six Realms, who also happened to be my personal enemy, didn't sit well with me.

Not just acquainted, I corrected myself, King Damien was married to her brother, which made her brother King Casimir. He wasn't just missing, he was dead. Killed by his own husband.

But he couldn't be her brother, he couldn't be because that would make her a...

"Princess?" I breathed out. She couldn't be. She would have told me.

She still had her eyes on the door.

"What?"

"Princess," I repeated, not able to form other words.

Her eyes moved back to mine. "Yes, love?"

"No, you're a princess."

She looked surprised, and then seeing the comprehension on my face, resigned herself to nodding. "I tried to tell you."

"When?!"

She smiled sheepishly. "When we first met."

I thought back and glared at her. "You most certainly didn't!" *Technically, she had said it, but still.* "You didn't try all that hard. Gods Lor, you're actually a princess? You're the lost Princess of Bancroft?"

Oh gods, my wife is from Bancroft. My wife and family were literally on opposite sides of a war. If I ever got to leave this place and visit home, the reunion was going to be interesting.

She gave me a small, sad smile "Technically, the hidden Princess of Bancroft. I'm not exactly lost. I'm so sorry, love. I didn't know who I could and couldn't trust. I had been keeping my secret for so long I didn't know how to stop, but this doesn't change anything."

I just looked at her. "Doesn't change anything?"

She frowned and took my hands. "Of course it doesn't. You have to know it doesn't change anything. I love you and I trust you, but with my brother gone, it wasn't safe for anyone to know. Plus, I loved being normal for once. I love our life here. This doesn't change anything."

"It changes a whole lot for me." She looked at me with a pain that startled me.

"I'm Altean."

She gasped. "I'm so sorry. I didn't know."

"I don't you didn't. I kept it from you to keep you safe. I thought if the Bancroftians found me, if they tortured me for information, you not knowing would keep you safe. Gods Lor, I've hated the Bancroftians ever since I had to leave my family, hated them for what they are doing to my Realm, to my family, and now I'm married to their Princess? We're supposed to hate each other. Your King, your brother-in-law is slaughtering my people."

She blanched at that. "It's been years since I've seen Damien, ever since my brother went missing." She swallowed hard, holding back tears and continued, "Damien hasn't been the same since Cass was taken. I can't pretend to know what's in his heart, but with him targeting Altea, he must believe the Alteans have Cass."

"But Cass is dead. Damien murdered him."

She shook her head vehemently. "Say whatever else you like about Damien, but he loved my brother more than life itself. He never would have harmed him. I wasn't there when the invasion happened, but I believe Damien. Cass was taken, and from the voracity of his attacks on Altea, he must believe Altea is holding Cass captive."

"He truly thinks that? To what end? What good is a kidnapped King without a ransom demand or a forced alliance?"

"I truly don't know, but I swear to you, we will find a way to stop him."

Some of the built-up tension flooded out of me now. "You would stand against him?"

"I would stand with my wife," she said, making my smile tentatively return. "Besides, Damein and I want the same thing, to find my brother. If it weren't for my pact with Cass, I would be out there looking for him, too. But if Altea didn't take him, who did?" she asked almost to herself.

"Maybe you could try asking your nephew about it?"

She blanched, her smile disappearing, "I can't risk it. There's a chance he would kill me on sight. Besides, I'm supposed to be staying away from anyone who might know me. I can't risk it."

"You can't risk it...? What are we even doing in Somerset if you're supposed to be in hiding? Being right here, under the nose of the royal family?" I would have laughed if I wasn't so worried. "I mean, gods Lor, you couldn't have picked a worse place to hide unless you had just stayed in Bancroft."

Her eyes were watering, but I heard her musical laugh and couldn't help but smile.

"You're not wrong. I've been running ever since my brother disappeared, ever since I turned. I kept bouncing from town to town, running from my past... until I ran into you. I was just passing through Somerset, so really this is your fault."

She grinned playfully before looking over toward the door again, listening. I didn't hear anything.

She looked at me and said, "We have a few more minutes, and I don't think he would recognize me, but you should probably take over the desk until he leaves."

I couldn't help but laugh. "Now that you're a fancy princess you're too good for desk work?"

She grinned. "If I had known there would be perks, I would've told you way sooner."

"Anything to get out of work, right, love?"

We both laughed a moment before her face fell. I studied her, knowing she was being pulled into her thoughts where it would be hard to reach her, so I asked her the first thing that came to my mind, "So if it wasn't Altea, which it wasn't, what do you think happened to your brother?"

I regretted asking the moment I saw the smile drop from her face.

"We're sure it wasn't Altea?"

"Positive. My parents are trusted advisors to the Queens. They would have known if it was us, we would have been prepared, but we weren't. When the first attack came, it was a slaughter."

"I'm so sorry, love. I know you might not believe me, but that's not the Damien I knew."

I sighed. She was right that I didn't believe her, but I knew she wasn't lying. She believed herself. I wasn't convinced, but knew we weren't going to get anywhere arguing about it, so instead I asked again, "So since it wasn't Altea. What do you think happened to your brother?"

"I don't know. Him and I had always planned for something like this. Our family is powerful, or was. We thought this might happen. Most of our lives, we had always been looking over our shoulders. I don't know who got him or how to get him back. Gods, I feel so helpless. If I still had my powers, I might be more useful, but that wasn't the plan."

"What do you mean?"

"Him and I had a deal." She smiled ruefully. "Whoever outlasted the other needed to be around long enough to avenge them. It was a sacrifice I never expected to have to make. I didn't think for a second anyone would be dumb enough to come after Cass. I always thought it would be me they hunted. We made a pact to ensure they wouldn't get us both."

She saw the confused look on my face and explained, "His magic was linked to mine, and mine to his. He could have been used to easily find me without even having to perform a spell. I could have tracked him down, too. I should have, but I kept my word."

"You have magic?" I asked shock evident in my voice. Before she could say anything else, a more pressing thought came to mind. "But if he can track you down, then you're still in danger."

She shook her head sadly. "I'm not. I sacrificed any chance I had of finding him, of saving him, to keep my promise to him. I sacrificed a piece of me when I turned. Vampires and magic don't mix."

I looked at her in awe. "So you let yourself be turned knowing you would have to give up your magic?"

She nodded. "I had to. I promised him. He would never have forgiven me if they got us both, if they used him to get to me. I couldn't make him live with that even if it killed me. Giving up my powers damn near did kill me, because not only did I give up my powers, but my link to him. I used to be able to just know how he was doing, what he was feeling, but not anymore. It's like I lost a piece of myself."

Tears started to fall down her face.

"I don't even know if he's still alive, never mind how he's feeling. If I didn't miss him this much, I would curse him for that stupid promise. I know that he's out there somewhere, smugly satisfied that even though he couldn't protect himself, he was able to protect me. Gods, I hate him for it. It should've been me."

My own tears fell as I pulled her into my arms.

"I'm so, so incredibly sorry. I can't believe you've been suffering through this all on your own."

"Well, I'm not alone now," she said softly.

"Nor will you ever be," I agreed. "Me and you, Lor, you're mine and I'm yours."

"Wholly and completely." She pulled back and kissed me. Even now, her kisses still stole my breath away.

She pulled back, listening again. "They'll be here any minute now."

I looked around the mess of a kitchen, itching to straighten things up. I couldn't think straight and staying busy helped, but it could wait.

"I can't believe you've been dealing with this all by yourself. You're even stronger than I gave you credit for."

She shrugged slightly. "It's been hard, but I can't even imagine how bad things have been for Damien."

"The King Killer?"

She rolled her eyes. "Stop calling him that. He had nothing to do with my brother's disappearance. Although it seems like I'm the only one in Zanaria who believes that."

"How do you know he wasn't involved?"

She shrugged. "I just do. You ought to have seen the way he looked at my brother, like Cass was a god among mortals." She laughed. "Damien worshipped him, like my brother needed any reason to have a bigger ego." She laughed before adding, "I haven't been able to speak with Damien since I ran. I don't even know if he would still speak to me if I tried. I don't know how he could possibly forgive me for abandoning him and throwing away our best chance of finding Cass. Even if I could safely contact him, I don't think he would want to talk to me."

"You mean you haven't heard?"

"Heard what?"

"King Damien is stuck in Sherbrooke."

"What? No. He can't be."

"He was supposed to marry Princess Serena."

She shook her head. "You have to be wrong. He wouldn't marry someone else, not with my brother out there waiting to be saved. It can't be him."

"Maybe I'm wrong, but I heard he went to the castle just before the curse struck."

"But that would mean..."

I nodded. "It would mean he's been in an enchanted sleep for the last few months."

She shook her head quicker now, "It can't be him. He's still out there looking for Cass. He would tear Zanaria apart piece by piece to find him if that's what it took."

Maybe I was wrong, but I didn't think so.

Before I could say anything else, I heard the horses. Enough hoofbeats that I knew we were out of time.

I kissed her quickly before saying, "Go. I'll meet you in our room as soon as I can get away."

She hesitated a moment, so I added, "I'll be fine. I can handle a spoiled Prince and his entourage."

She laughed. "That's what I'm worried about. I don't need you being condemned to death for your special brand of customer service."

I laughed at that, protesting, "I'm not that bad!"

She just cocked her eyebrow at me, amusement dancing in her eyes.

I held up my hands in defense. "Okay, okay. I'll behave. I promise."

She laughed and stole one more quick kiss before rushing out toward our room.

I heard the front door barge open and took a deep breath, stealing myself for what was coming.

Well, this ought to be interesting.

I shouldn't have been surprised. Life with Loralie was proving to be many things, but boring wasn't one of them.

I brushed the remaining flour off myself and rushed toward the entryway, only to find the door to the kitchen wouldn't budge. With a groan I remembered the faulty doorhandle I had Char fix earlier this week. I wasn't sure what he had done to it, but clearly it wasn't fixed. Of all the days, I thought with a groan.

The Prince wouldn't be happy to be kept waiting and the last thing I or Lor needed was to give them reason to look closer at the Sapphire Siren Inn.

I tried the handle once more before abandoning hope and rushing out the back. If I was quick and careful, I could make it around front and through the side entrance off the garden in time to beat them to the desk.

I barreled around the side of the Inn to the front, halting in my tracks at the corner, seeing a tall blonde gentleman standing aside an angry looking woman. There was something regal about his stance and I knew without a doubt he was Prince Tristan.

I wanted to sidle past them and make it inside unnoticed, but their hushed tones made me curious and cautious.

"If you think I care what you want, you're a good deal stupider than my betrothed." she spat out, low, but loud enough I heard.

I couldn't believe she was talking to the Prince like that. I paid slightly more attention to her now. She was quite short, made shorter looking by the Prince who was a good deal taller than her. She had soft chestnut waves that had been tangled from what looked to have been a long journey. The hem of her dress was in tatters. I took a closer look at the Prince then, and noticed what I had missed before. He didn't look much better. His tunic had rips in it that weren't Princely in appearance.

He looked frustrated and grabbed her wrist. She yanked it away a moment later saying, "Stupid must run in the family."

His composure snapped at that and he bit back, "You're hardly a picnic. Why any man would choose you for his bride is beyond me."

She glowered at him.

If she had a retort, it was drowned out by hoofbeats. I had been surprised that he was travelling alone with a lady, so I wasn't startled to see five soldiers on horses coming from around the other side of the Inn and five more heading in the direction of the stables.

One of the soldiers hopped off his horse and approached the still bickering Prince and the woman. The Prince, noticing the soldier approaching, straightened to his full height and adopted a smile. She just crossed her arms and rolled her eyes. I decided then that I liked her.

The guard bowed low to the Prince, who watched him, waiting. The woman's eyes followed the Prince, watching him with a guarded curiosity. I smirked at that. When he finished speaking with the guard and looked back at her, she scowled again. He didn't bat an eye before gesturing at her to go ahead. She had only taken a single step before his eyes were glued to her, watching the way she moved. I grinned, wondering if either of them noticed the other's attention. I doubted it. Maybe I could have a little fun with this. After all, it wasn't every day royalty came to stay. Why not help make it a night they would remember? I held back my laughter, but it died in me a moment later when I realized they were heading to the front desk and I wasn't there.

I quickly went over the options before turning back the way I had come, sprinting around the Inn to the garden door the long way. They might be kept waiting, but it was that or be caught eavesdropping and I didn't want to find out if eavesdropping on royalty in Somerset was a punishable crime.

I made it through the garden door in time to see the guards come spilling into the room with the Prince and the woman in the midst of their swarm. I wondered what took them so long, but heard one of the guards mention the stables taking forever with the horses. I was glad for once that the Inn didn't run its own stables. I didn't envy the townsfolk who kept the Prince's guards waiting.

The guards eyed me suspiciously until I stepped behind the counter. They checked the room and gave me a once over before nodding to the Prince. He approached the desk and gave me a smile that I was sure would have had half the kingdom swooning.

"I apologize for our rather dramatic entrance. I hope we won't be causing you much trouble requesting your best room with two beds, and the rest of your rooms for our entourage," he said with a sheepish smile handing me a bag weighted down with what felt to be gold.

The Winter Solstice Festival had just ended a couple of days ago, so we had a few days break from guests and I was easily able to accommodate his request. How interesting that he wanted her in the same room, though. I looked her and the Prince over and decided whoever she was, she was definitely out of his league, Prince or not. No wonder he wanted to keep her close. I wondered if she was actually engaged to one of his family members, but the thought confused me. News of a royal wedding would've been the talk of the town and I hadn't heard anything. Maybe it was distant cousin to the Prince she was supposed to marry. I wondered if the cousin had any idea how clearly close the Prince and the woman were. I wondered what brought them here.

I knew I should just accommodate his request, but seeing the way they looked at each other, I couldn't stop myself. Clearly, she shouldn't be marrying his cousin if she was looking at him like that and it might take ages for them to get out of their own way and figure that out.

Fortunately, I was in the position to speed up the process. I was going to have fun with this. They'd thank me one day. Maybe they'd even name the little Princeling or Princess after me. I fought to keep in my laughter. I easily could have moved a second bed into one of the larger rooms, but where was the fun in that?

I tried to look contrite as I said, "I'm sorry, Your Highness, the only rooms we have here are rooms with one bed."

His smile faltered for just a moment. He glanced over at her to see her scowling at him. This was going to be entertaining. He smirked at her as he turned back to me and said, "That'll have to do. The lady and I can share."

The look of shock on her face made him look much more smug. I was fighting so hard to keep the laughter in that my eyes were watering. I was careful to make sure I gave the Prince and his entourage the right keys, all but two.

I had thought I was being discreet, but the Prince noticed. "Good lady, I should hope you won't allow other guests while we're here. You should know I highly respect my privacy, and pay well for it." He gestured to the gold he had handed over.

I bowed my head. "Of course not, Your Highness. Consider the Inn closed until your party leaves." He eyed the leftover keys and raised his eyebrows. Stifling a sigh, I said, "One of them is to my own chambers."

"And the second?" he asked.

My eyes darkened. "The second is not for guests."

"What, pray tell, is it for?"

My eyes darkened even more. Did he know? He couldn't possibly. "Storage," was all I said.

He nodded. That seemed to appease him. He thanked me and was swept out of the room amid his soldiers, the woman begrudgingly shuffling behind him.

Once it was clear they didn't need anything else from me, I rushed up to our room to check in on Lor and catch her up to speed. I knew she was probably dying to know what was going on.

When I opened the door, I was startled to see Lor having tea and biscuits with Char while Coal sat across the room lapping milk from a small teacup.

"What-" I started, but Lor interrupted, which was for the best since my brain was malfunctioning and I didn't even know what to ask.

"I met Char in the entryway on my way up here, with a basket full of sweets. You know I can't resist sweets."

"Or my Char-ms." Char said, waggling his eyebrows, "get it? Char-ms."

I laughed despite myself.

"So is the Prince really here?" he asked.

"Him, half the royal guard, and a woman he very clearly has a thing for."

As worried as I knew Lor was, I knew she couldn't resist a good love story. She loved playing matchmaker, so when I told her about their sleeping arrangements, both her and Char were impressed.

Coal wasn't, but he wasn't easy to impress, unless you were Loralie. He was obsessed with her, unlike me he thought she could do no wrong.

I sat with them on the rug, Char scooted over to make room for me and we took turns making up stories about how we thought the Prince and his mystery woman were going to spend their night together.

I just hoped they managed not to kill each other, the Inn had seen too much murder already. We were turning over a new leaf at the Sapphire Siren Inn. It was officially a murder-free zone thanks to my lovely vampire wife and I couldn't have been happier about it. As I lounged in our room with my wife, my meddlesome best friend Char, and my troublesome cat Coal, I couldn't help thinking that with them by my side, even with me being cursed to stay here, the Sapphire Siren Inn felt like home.

THE END

So, what did you think of Under Lock and Key?

I would love to hear any and all of your thoughts! If you would be so kind as to leave any review it would be greatly appreciated. Any review, good or bad, short or long, is always welcome.

For updates on my next book or to tell me what you thought about this one, you can find me:

Visit my website: Thelibraryofsarahzane.com

Or follow me on TikTok or Instagram: Libraryofsarahzane

Like my Facebook page: Sarah Zane (libraryofsarahzane)

Please come find me on any of those platforms, I would love to hear what you thought about my book!

ABOUT THE AUTHOR

 Sarah is an author of happy endings for traumatized queers.

She is a bisexual feminist and a licensed therapist. Her stories deal with themes of feminism, trauma, sexuality, and mental health.

She lives in New England with her 2 black cats named Gatsby and Mr. Darcy. When she isn't writing, she can be found perusing a book in her home library, making chaotic book themed videos for TikTok (aka Booktok), taking forest walks, visiting castles, planning exotic trips she can't afford, or cuddled up with one of her cats crying over fictional characters yelling at them about how badly they need therapy.

For more from Sarah Zane, check out...

Beautiful Little Fool

A sapphic, feminist retelling of the Great Gatsby from Daisy's POV.

Sequel coming December 2024...

Off Script: A Book Ball Fantasy Adventure

A fantasy adventure story about Sadie, a fantasy author whose first convention goes haywire when her characters literally jump off the page.

Cosplay and Confrontation

A sapphic rivals-to-lovers cosplayers romcom that takes place at the same fantasy convention in *Off Script.*

Acknowledgements

First, I want to thank Jess for being a huge support and cheerleader for my author career. Your advice and support are invaluable and without your encouragement this story certainly wouldn't have existed in this form. Your encouragement to stay true to my voice and write what I want has been instrumental. I appreciate you more than I can express.

To Erica, thank you for beta-ing the story and loving Del and Lor as much as I do. Your excitement over it got me to continue working on and perfecting the story. You're a large reason it's been elevated to what it is now and I appreciate you so much.

To Marissa for writing *Between Mischief and Magic* and showing me that sapphic cozy fantasy stories can do well and for encouraging me to not give up on writing one of my own.

To My Leos, thank you for being there for me through everything and for continuing to be there for me. I adore you both more than I can express.

To my family and friends, thank you all so much for the love and support. It means more to me than I can express. There are way too many of you to list here, but know I appreciate you.

Thank you to my beloved Booktok community of wonderful authors, readers, and new friends. I have so much love for you all and am incredibly happy to have found such a great community that makes me feel so at home.

Last but not least, thank you to you, dear reader, for reading this and helping support my crazy dream of being an author.

From the bottom of my heart, I love you all.

www.ingramcontent.com/pod-product-compliance
Lightning Source LLC
Chambersburg PA
CBHW061547310726
48972CB00008B/2648